Invincible Summer

Books by Jean Ferris

Amen, Moses Gardenia

The Stainless Steel Rule

Invincible Summer

Invincible Summer

JEAN FERRIS

Farrar Straus Giroux
NEW YORK

Excerpt from "Morning Has Broken" by Eleanor
Farjeon, copyright 1957 by Eleanor Farjeon, re-
printed by permission of Harold Ober Associates
Incorporated. "Goodbye World," excerpt from *Our
Town* by Thornton Wilder, copyright 1938, 1957
by Thornton Wilder, reprinted by permission of
Harper & Row, Publishers, Inc.

*To the memory of my father
and of Bertha Mae Weatherford*

Summer

On a well-planned farm, as Will Gregory's was, the most important view is the one from the kitchen window. From there, everything—the farmyard, the barn, the workshop, the storage sheds, the silo, the lanes leading to the fields—can be seen.

Robin's first memory was the view from that window as she sat on the counter while her mother, humming, put up the products of her kitchen garden—tomatoes and watermelon-rind preserves, beans and pickled cucumber, raspberry jam. Years later, Robin still found herself listening for that humming.

It was to the same window that her father's eyes turned often, as they did now, even during a meal, to watch the sky, always gauging the weather, in the never-ending assessment of what it would mean to his crops.

As Robin sat picking at her food, the flat orange rays of the sun reached through the window over the sink, between the starched blue-edged curtains, and stretched across the scrubbed kitchen until they collided with a glass of water on the supper table in an explosion of light. Robin winced. She already had a headache.

"I have to go up and change now, Libby." Robin pushed her chair back from the table.

"You hardly ate anything. Are you feeling all right?" her grandmother asked.

"I feel okay. It's the heat, I guess. I just don't have much appetite."

"You're right about the heat. Isn't this awful, Will? When's the last time you remember the first day of June being so hot?"

Robin's father looked up from his plate. "Never," he said. "I hope that hybrid corn I've got in is as drought-resistant as they say." He glanced at the window again before turning back to his dinner.

"Where you going tonight, Robin?" Libby asked.

"We're going to town to the movies."

"You and Ivan?"

"Who else?"

"Been a while since you've been out with anybody but him, hasn't it?" Libby asked.

"Once you start going out with somebody, nobody else asks you. That's how it works."

"That's not the way we did it. The more beaux you had, the better." Libby began gathering up the thick white everyday dishes and carrying them to the sink. "You tell him to drive slower," she said. "I've seen him barreling down the highway in that pickup. It's seven miles from here to town and that's plenty of room to get in trouble. That boy's got a wild streak, just like his daddy and his big brother."

"Oh, Libby. Ivan's just . . . high-spirited. He's been like that since we were little." She wasn't sure why she was defending him. It was almost like a reflex: that's the way girls with boyfriends were supposed to act. She'd learned that from Marci. Ivan was the first boy Robin had gone out with long enough to have to use Marci's instructions, and sometimes it seemed Marci was more thrilled by their dating than Robin was herself.

To tell the truth, Ivan's driving scared Robin, too. But she dismissed that as normal overreacting for someone whose mother had been killed in an automobile accident.

"Anyway," she continued, "everybody drives fast around here. That's practically all there is to do. Do *you* always keep to the speed limit on the way to town?"

Libby flicked a dish towel at her and laughed. "Go on and get changed. I'm an old lady. There's not too many vices left for me. Tell him to slow down. You hear?"

"Okay, okay," Robin said as she went up the back stairs from the kitchen to her bedroom.

The farmhouse, which had been built by her great-grandfather, was almost one hundred years old, but had been modernized over the years, especially under her mother's direction. As a bride Julie had insisted on a new kitchen and bathrooms and on central air-conditioning. It was expensive but soybean prices were high that year and Julie helped pay for it with the money she earned teaching school in town.

Without the air-conditioning, it would have been unbearable in the house now. It was at least an hour until sunset, when some cooling could be expected, though for the past week the nights, too, had been unseasonably warm. Robin couldn't imagine how her great-grandmother had lived and worked in this house during the scorching Iowa summers.

Robin's heart was pounding and her upper lip was

glossed with sweat when she got to the top of the stairs. She went to her room and lay on the bed to catch her breath, thinking what lousy shape she must be in.

"Robin, Ivan's here." Libby stood in the doorway of Robin's room, outlined by the fading light of dusk. "Why, you haven't even started getting ready."

Robin sat up on her bed. "Oh, my gosh, I must have fallen asleep."

"I'll say." Libby turned on a light. "Look at your face! You've got candlewick marks on you from the bedspread. You could stay home tonight, you know, if you're tired. Tell Ivan those bumps are something contagious."

"No," Robin said. "I'm okay. Anyway, he'd be mad if I broke a date this late."

"In that case," Libby said with a note of disapproval, "you better get moving. I'll go give Ivan a lecture about safe driving. Anyway, if I don't get downstairs and make some kind of conversation, he and your dad'll just sit there looking at each other like two cigar-store Indians." She turned and left the room, closing the door behind her.

Robin hurriedly changed clothes and brushed her hair. She knew no amount of makeup could hide the bedspread marks on her face, so she didn't even try.

When she came down the stairs into the front parlor, Ivan looked at her with relief and jumped to his feet.

"Sorry I'm late," she said. "I fell asleep."

"We better hurry if we're going to make the show. Good night, Mr. Gregory, Mrs. Clayton." Ivan flung open the front door, took Robin's hand, and pulled her across the screened-in porch and down the front steps to his truck.

"Take it easy," Robin said. "We've got enough time."

"You *know* how I hate it when you're not ready," he said. "Your father sits there like a zombie, and if I ask him a question or anything, he answers with one word. And your grandmother, she won't shut up. Now I'm supposed to drive to town at ten miles an hour to keep her off my back!" He slammed the truck into gear and roared out of the gravel driveway, the radio blaring. Robin looked over her shoulder and saw Libby standing at the door to the porch, hands on her hips.

"You sick or something? Most girls wouldn't be going to sleep when they were supposed to be getting ready for a date. Especially with me." He laughed.

"I'm just tired from the heat. I lay down for a minute, and when Libby woke me up, it was an hour later."

"Well, don't do it again," he said, taking his hand from the wheel and closing it over hers. She glanced at the speedometer, where the needle quivered at seventy-five. "I like the way you look, fresh out of bed," he said, his voice softer. "It's sexy."

She pulled her hand away and lifted his back onto the steering wheel. "Please," she said.

"I wish we hadn't told Marci and Bobby we'd meet them at the movies. The way you look, it makes me want to . . ."

"I've been looking forward to seeing this movie," Robin interrupted. "It's supposed to be great. And I really like Meryl Streep." She chattered on about the movie, knowing she was trying to distract Ivan. As she talked, she looked at his big blond head, silhouetted against the window in the dark cab of the truck. The headlights of cars speeding in the opposite direction briefly illuminated his features and she could see him smiling to himself. What was he thinking about? Her? His truck? Football? She'd known him since she was four and she still had few clues to the way his mind worked. If it was working at all, she sometimes thought.

When they got to Bennett, Ivan screeched into a parking place on Main Street in front of the hardware store. They hurried the half block to the theater, Robin trotting to keep up with him. Marci and Bobby waited on the sidewalk, nuzzling against each other.

"Come *on,* you two," said Marci. "The picture's about to start. Hey, Robin, what happened to your face?"

"It's from my bedspread. I fell asleep after dinner."

"Must be pretty exciting, getting ready to go out with Ivan," Bobby said. Ivan pretended to take a swing at him and the boys started shadow-boxing.

"Will you guys knock it off," Marci said. "I don't want to miss the beginning."

As they entered the darkened theater, Ivan slid his arm around Robin's waist and whispered, "What do you say, Rob? Why don't we sit in the back row?" He kissed her ear.

"I . . . let's sit with Marci and Bobby," she said. What she chose to do with Ivan in the truck after the movie was her own business; she didn't want to do it in the theater and make it everybody else's, too.

Sullenly he followed Bobby and Marci down the aisle. But as they sat in the dark watching the movie, Ivan reached his arm around Robin's shoulders and pulled her against him, and her stomach quivered. Even when she was irritated with him, she couldn't help the way he made her feel. She had a hard time concentrating on the picture while he was touching her.

When the movie was over, Robin knew they would go to the Crest Café for something to eat. That's what they always did after the movies. That's what everybody always did after the movies in Bennett. But first they would go to the ladies' room. They always did that after the movies, too.

"Why don't you let your hair grow longer, Rob?" Marci asked, standing before the mirror making minute adjustments to her own long hair. "It's so nice and thick, there should be more of it."

Robin ran her fingers through her shoulder-length hair. "It gets too messy. It looks awful long."

"I'm glad to see old Ivan's growing his hair out. I hated him with a crew cut. He looks great tonight, don't you think?"

"He always looks good. That's the problem. It worries me we have so little to say to each other, but usually when we're alone I could care less about talking."

"So? You like that part, don't you?"

"Yes—but it seems so . . . so impersonal."

"That's about as personal as you can get, for goodness' sakes! Don't worry, you'll get to know each other better the more you go out. And having a date every Saturday night is nothing to sneeze at." Marci put on fresh lipstick. "Or would you rather sit at home playing Parcheesi with Libby?" She cocked her head at her reflection in the mirror.

"I don't think that would bother me the way it would

you. It's just that I thought having a boyfriend would be more . . . more . . . I don't know—more *something*."

"Well, you have to work with them, you know, like training an animal. It takes a while. Look at Bobby. A month ago he thought he could go out with Mary Ann Peters and me at the same time. I changed his mind about *that* in a hurry."

Robin wished she had more of Marci's certainty about how things were supposed to be. But she also wished Marci wasn't so settled and content with the small pleasures and intrigues Bennett had to offer. She needed someone to share her restlessness. In spite of how long they'd been best friends, from habit now as much as from growing up together, they didn't look at the future the same way at all. Robin saw every day as a day closer to the one she would leave Bennett. To Marci, each day was another bead on a chain of days all the same.

Marci linked her arm through Robin's as they walked through the theater lobby to join the boys outside. Robin felt guilty, and grateful for her friend's steady affection.

Outside, Ivan separated them. "I get her now," he said to Marci, taking Robin's hand and leading her through the warm darkness. When they entered the air-conditioned Crest Café, Robin shivered.

"Cold?" Ivan asked, putting his arm around her. She shivered again. He held her tighter. "Come on, sit in this booth. I'll keep you warm."

The four of them slid into the booth, and Ivan pressed against Robin. It embarrassed her to have him so close, but Marci winked across the table at her and Bobby seemed preoccupied with the menu.

"Hi, Nikki," Robin said to the waitress, who was also the best basketball player in Robin's PE class.

"Hi," Nikki said, cracking her gum explosively. "What can I get you?"

Marci ordered a Diet Coke and Robin ordered orange juice.

"I'll have a piece of pie," Bobby said. "What kind do you have?"

"Apple, cherry, lemon meringue, chocolate and banana cream," Nikki said, punctuating the list with small detonations.

"I'll have cherry. À la mode. What kind of ice cream do you have?"

"Vanilla, chocolate, rocky road, butter pecan, burgundy cherry; rainbow, lemon and orange sherbet."

"I'll have vanilla."

She turned to Ivan. "How about you?"

"I'll have pie, too."

"What kind?"

"What have you got?"

"You heard me before," she said with a vicious snap of her gum. "What kind do you want?"

"I forgot."

"Apple, cherry, lemon meringue, chocolate and banana cream."

"I'll have cherry."

Nikki wrote on her pad. "Anything else?"

"Yeah," Ivan said. "I think I'll have my pie à la mode. Do you have any ice cream?"

Nikki just looked at him.

"Are you being obnoxious, or what?" Marci asked.

"What about the ice cream?" Ivan asked.

Nikki rolled her eyes to the ceiling and shifted her gum to the other cheek. "Vanilla, chocolate, butter pecan, rocky road, burgundy cherry."

"Any sherbet?" Ivan asked.

"Ivan!" Robin said.

"What are you trying to prove?" asked Marci.

Bobby grinned.

Nikki stood holding her pad. "Okay, wise guy. What'll it be?"

"What about the sherbet?"

"Rainbow, lemon, and orange, Dr. Einstein."

"Hey, can't you take a little joke?" Ivan asked. He turned to Bobby. "The girl has no sense of humor."

"That's *enough*, Ivan," Robin said. "Just order, okay?"

"I'll have vanilla." Nikki wrote it down and left.

"What did you do that for?" Robin asked.

"It was just in fun," Ivan said. "No big deal."

"Well, I think it was mean." She slumped against the wall of the booth, away from Ivan.

"Robin's right," Marci said. "You guys acted like jerks. How do you think Nikki felt?"

"I don't know," Ivan said. "I didn't feel her." The boys looked at each other and snickered. Marci gave Robin a disgusted look and shook her head like the mother of two naughty children.

Nikki brought the drinks and pie, deposited them, and left without speaking.

The girls sipped their drinks, ignoring the boys, who were having such a good time insulting each other that they paid no attention. When they were finished, the girls went outside, where it was still humid and warm, while the boys paid the check.

"I hope they left her a big tip," Marci said. "What jerks."

"They were infantile," Robin said. "I don't know why Nikki didn't drop the pie in their laps."

Bobby came out first, took Marci's hand, and started off down the sidewalk toward his car. "Now for the good part," he said. Marci looked back over her shoulder and said to Robin, "Call me in the morning."

Ivan held the back of Robin's neck in his big hand as he steered her toward the truck. "Aw, come on. It was all in fun. You're taking this too serious."

"It may have been fun for you guys, but I doubt Nikki enjoyed it much."

"She was cool. You mind more than she did."

"I thought it was humiliating."

They reached the truck and Ivan opened the door for Robin. "All right. I'm sorry. I acted like a dope. I *am* a dope. I'm the biggest dope in the world. Are you satisfied? Will you stop being mad?"

"Well . . . okay. Just don't forget you're a dope."

"Never. I'll never forget it. How can I when I have you to remind me?"

He got into the truck and they sped down the highway with the air-conditioning and the music both on high.

"You know what I like best about this long road up to your house?" he asked.

"What?"

"How dark and lonesome it is this time of night. How

I can park next to the hedge by that old walnut tree just up the road from your house and nobody can see we're there."

Ivan pulled the truck in under the tree and turned out the lights. He left the ignition on so the air-conditioning and the music wouldn't stop, though he lowered them both. Then he put his arm around her. Automatically she turned her face to him, ready for his kiss.

Robin felt as if she was sinking underwater, the way she had done as a little girl in the community pool. She would sit on the bottom of the pool with her eyes closed and listen to the far-off reverberations of sound through the water. Her fair floated around her face and she felt light-headed and dreamy.

Ivan put his hand on Robin's breast. She pulled away from him, her faraway feeling shattered.

"Don't."

"Why not? We've been going out for two months and making out like maniacs under this tree every time. You seem to enjoy it as much as I do. You keep going out with me. What am I supposed to think? Or are you just a tease?"

"I don't want you to, that's all."

"Well, *excuse* me. You care to tell me why?" His face was so close to her she could feel his breath on her cheek.

"I guess I'm just not ready. I like you, Ivan, but I don't want to go any farther right now." She leaned a little away from him.

He took his arm from around her shoulders and held on to the steering wheel. "Then you mean we won't be going out anymore."

"I didn't say that."

"Sorry, babe. There's plenty of other girls who'll let me and like it. I can't hold back forever. I've been more patient with you than with any girl I've ever been out with."

"You mean they all let you do whatever you want to?"

"I always had the feeling they wanted to, too."

"Oh." But she didn't want to. She didn't like the way it made her feel intruded upon, forced into something too important to share with someone she felt as ambivalent about as Ivan.

"Aw, come on, Robin," he said, putting his arm around her again. "It's not that big a deal. Everybody does it."

"I'm sorry. I can't." She knew she meant it, but at the same time she wished she didn't. She wanted, at that moment, to be like everybody else.

He shrugged. "Okay. If that's how it is." He started the truck and turned the music up again.

Ivan stopped the truck in the driveway by the front porch, reached across Robin, and opened her door. "See you around. Let me know if you change your mind."

She jumped down from the truck and ran to the house as he roared away. She took a pillow from the new wicker love seat on the porch and threw it as hard as she could through the open front door into the hall. When she went to retrieve it, thinking guiltily of how long Libby had saved to buy the new porch furniture, she saw Libby sitting in the parlor, knitting.

"Does that mean you didn't have a good time?" Libby asked.

Robin flopped down on the couch next to her, hugging the pillow. "Yes."

"You want to tell me about it?"

Robin listened to the peaceful clicking of Libby's knitting needles. "Ivan wanted to do something I didn't want to do. And now he doesn't want to go out with me anymore."

"Which are you more, sad or mad?"

"I don't know. Both, I guess. I liked having a boyfriend, even if it was just Ivan. But I didn't like the way he wanted to push me. And I hate having *him* decide he doesn't want to see *me* anymore. I wanted to be the one to decide that."

"Yes. That's nice, that kind of choice. Are you going to miss him?"

"I suppose. But I think what I'll miss most is being one of the girls with a boyfriend—it's such proof that you're normal."

"Don't worry. You did the right thing. You were true to yourself, and that counts. Believe me, I know what I'm talking about. I had two bum marriages, trying to please somebody else. It wasn't until I figured out what *I* wanted that I got a good one."

"Do you think anybody'll ever want to marry me?" She leaned her head against the back of the couch.

Libby stopped knitting. "Your mother used to ask me the same thing. And I'll tell you what I told her: only the most special man will do for you, but with luck you'll find him."

"Mama found her man. And in Bennett, too. I don't think there's anybody in Bennett for me."

"Well, I doubt you'll be in Bennett forever. Not you."

"I hope you're right. I'd want to lie down and die if I thought I'd never get out of here."

Libby patted Robin's knee and resumed her knitting.

"What are you making?" Robin asked.

"A sweater for you."

"Sweater! Don't even say that word in this weather."

"It won't last forever."

"It already seems like it's lasted forever." She stood up. "I'm dead. I have to go to bed." She stretched and kissed Libby on the cheek. "See you in the morning."

"Good night, doll baby. Talking to you tonight reminds me so much of the way your mother and I used to talk. It takes me back."

Robin kissed Libby again and went upstairs to bed.

She lay thinking about Ivan and trying to find a comfortable position. She thought she'd go right to sleep, she was so tired, but she couldn't relax. She wondered if she was getting the flu; she felt achy and maybe a little feverish. It was probably just the weather upsetting her system. Ivan had upset her system, too.

Unquestionably, he was a jerk. He'd proved that tonight. More than once. Still, she knew she wouldn't like it when she saw him walking down the hall at school with his arm around another girl. She was surprised to find tears welling up and overflowing, sliding from the corners of her eyes into her pillow.

Robin heard Libby come up the stairs and close the door to her room. She had the big bedroom now with its own sitting room and bath, the bedroom that used to be

Will's and Julie's. After Julie died, Will refused to sleep there. He moved into the small bedroom across the hall, the one separated from Robin's by a bathroom, which they shared.

She wiped her tears with the corner of the sheet and hoped Libby was right about getting out of Bennett. Maybe for college. There was a lot she loved about Bennett—it was home, after all—but she wanted a life where something besides the harvest and the high school football games were the big events. And where she could meet someone unlike Ivan in every way.

"You taking up sleeping for your latest hobby?" Libby asked her.

Robin opened her eyes to find Libby standing by her bed. "Hi," she said groggily. "What time is it?"

"It's twelve-thirty. I've been to church and back, started the supper, and done three loads of wash. I even did your chores. That poor cow got tired of waiting for you to milk her, and the chickens were beating down the kitchen door for their breakfast."

Robin tried to smile, but her face felt too heavy to respond. In spite of her long sleep, she didn't feel rested.

"You all right?" Libby asked. She bent over Robin and felt her forehead. "Why, you're hot! I think you've got a temperature. I'm going to get the thermometer. You stay there."

"Don't worry," Robin said. She felt so slow and leaden she wondered if she could move at all.

Libby took Robin's temperature and it was 101. "No wonder! Do you hurt anywhere? Sore throat? Ear ache?"

"No. I just ache all over. My muscles hurt."

"It sounds like the flu. And with only one more week of school to go."

"And then exams. Don't forget exams."

"You won't have any trouble with exams even if you have to miss a few days of school. You always do fine. I'm going down to heat up some chicken soup and make Jell-O. You want anything else?"

"No." Even soup and Jell-O were more than she wanted.

Libby went downstairs and Robin made her way dizzily to the bathroom. By the time she got back to bed, she was exhausted.

Libby returned with a tray of toast, soup, and orange juice and put it on Robin's bedside table. "You want some help?"

"No. Just keep me company."

Libby pulled up the armchair, removing a pile of clothes, which she automatically sorted for the wash. "Here's why you can never find anything clean to wear." She sat down. "I hope you gave Ivan the flu last night. It would make a nice goodbye present. There've been a couple of times in my life when I've wished I had a good disease to give somebody."

"Your husbands before Herb?" Robin asked between sips of soup.

"The second one, for sure. Maybe not the first."

"Why did you get married so young the first time?" Robin couldn't imagine marrying at seventeen—her own age.

"Because I couldn't keep my hands off him. Or his off

me. In those days, when you felt like that, you had to
get married. Two years, one baby, and a lot of silences
later, we knew we'd never be able to live together. We
burned out on the physical stuff and he wasn't ready to
support a family, come home at night, save part of his
paycheck, all those real-life things. Then the baby got
pneumonia and died and that was the end. No reason for
us to stay together. He had a sweet face, though, and a
beautiful body, but I haven't missed him for one day since
we said goodbye. I haven't seen him for, oh, must be
over thirty years." She glanced at Robin, who had given
up on the soup and was leaning back on the pillow. "Look
at you, falling asleep while I yammer on." She stood and
picked up the tray. "You get some sleep. It's nature's
medicine."

Robin rolled over and was asleep before Libby was out
of the room.

When she opened her eyes again, a sunset light was in
her room. Her mouth was dry and she felt stiff and sore.
She tried to stretch, but it didn't help.

"How are you feeling?" her father asked. Robin hadn't
seen him sitting in the armchair in the shadows, tying
knots in a piece of baler twine, something he did when
he was troubled.

"Hi, Daddy. About the same, I guess. I was hoping I'd
be better."

"You need anything?"

"You can help me up. I have to go to the bathroom."

He helped her out of bed and she leaned against him

on the way to the bathroom. He was a big man, tall and broad, and his presence always reassured her.

When she was finished in the bathroom, he tucked her in and kissed her on the forehead.

"Be careful," she said. "You don't want to get sick. You've got too much to do."

He kissed her again. "Hungry?"

"No. Just tired."

"I'll sit here for a while if you want."

"I'd like that. Don't mind if I fall asleep again. It's nothing personal."

He smiled and sat down in the armchair.

She fell asleep.

The next time she woke, it was early morning. She wanted to feel better, but when she tried to get out of bed, she knew she was too weak and wobbly to go to school.

Libby was in her room when Robin came out of the bathroom. "How do you feel?"

"Lousy."

"School?"

She shook her head.

"Okay. Back to bed. I'll bring up breakfast."

Robin spent most of the day dozing and was disappointed to find that she still felt rotten when she woke up. But she was bored with illness, so she pulled on jeans and a T-shirt and made her way downstairs, where she sat on the sofa in the parlor until she fell asleep again. She joined Libby and Will in the kitchen for supper but didn't have much appetite, even though Libby had fixed her favorite dinner, macaroni and cheese with tomatoes, and oatmeal cookies.

After dinner, while Libby cleaned up the kitchen and Will went out to sharpen the cultivator shovels, Robin sat in the parlor, so exhausted she wondered if she'd be able to get upstairs to go to bed.

When the phone rang, it took effort for her to lift the receiver.

"Hi," Marci said. "Are you feeling better? I called a couple of times yesterday, but Libby said you were sick."

"I still feel pretty crummy. I hope I can get to school tomorrow."

"It might be a good idea."

"Why?"

"Ivan's telling everybody he dumped you Saturday night and you're so upset about it you can't come to school. Is that really why you're sick?"

"Why, that *rat!*"

"Well, come on, give. What happened?"

"He made a move on me, and when I told him no, he didn't like it. He said the only way he'd keep going out with me is if I gave in, and I wasn't about to."

"You can be sure Ivan'll never tell that story. How are you going to get him back?"

"Back? I don't want him back."

"Are you sure? Saturday nights can get awful lonely. And he likes you so much."

"I'm not sure he does anymore. Anyway, I'm not afraid of Saturday nights."

"Be real, Rob. Any boyfriend is better than none. Well,

almost any. I mean, there's always *somebody* who would be okay to go out with. At least it gives you something to do while you wait for Prince Charming."

"My Prince Charming's not in Bennett. I'm going to have to wait until I'm somewhere else to look." She lay down on the sofa and took the phone with her.

"I don't know why you're always so anxious to get out of Bennett. There's a lot of nice things here: church socials and 4H and hay rides."

"Oh, Marci, I like those things. I just want more."

"Well," Marci said, a baffled note in her voice, "I hope you find it." Then, sounding like herself again, "Do you think you'll be able to come to school tomorrow?"

"I'll come even if I'm dying. I want everybody to know Ivan has nothing to do with my being sick."

"Okay. I'll see you tomorrow. And look terrific, for goodness' sakes. Just in case Prince Charming's around."

The next morning Robin still felt achy and dizzy, but she put on makeup, dressed with care, and went to school. She'd show Ivan.

It wasn't easy. She couldn't concentrate and her eyes kept sliding closed. It took all her energy to drag herself from one class to another, and she couldn't focus on what people said to her.

Ivan passed her a couple of times in the hall but pretended he didn't see her, and she was too preoccupied with trying to make it through the day to impress him with how well she was doing without him.

She went straight to bed when she got home, was too tired to eat dinner, and fell asleep over her books.

She plodded through the next three days, determined to finish the year well. Grades good enough to qualify her for a college scholarship were her ticket to the world and she didn't intend to blow her future because of the flu.

Robin slept all the time she wasn't studying during the weekend but still wasn't feeling normal by Monday morning.

"No wonder you don't feel good yet," Libby scolded her. "When you're sick, you're supposed to lie down and take care of yourself until you feel better. If you get up and go to school and do homework and all that, you don't get better. Obviously." She put a plate of bacon, eggs, and toast in front of Robin. "Eat something."

Robin nibbled on some toast and had a few bites of egg. She could almost feel the circles under her eyes lying on her cheeks.

"When's your last exam?" Libby asked.

"Wednesday. Why?"

"I'm getting you an appointment with Dr. Paul for Wednesday afternoon. I don't like the way this is hanging on."

"What if I'm better by then?"

"I'll cancel the appointment. I hope I have to."

"I've got to go. I'll see you this afternoon."

Robin squinted at the words of her exam questions through burning eyes. Her head hurt and her thoughts refused to organize themselves. She labored through her tests, doing the best she could, but suspecting it wasn't very good. The only advantage of exam days was that they were shorter than regular school days.

On Wednesday, with weary relief, Robin got into her mother's old blue Honda and drove slowly home from school. She hadn't managed to arrange an encounter with Ivan where she could be cool yet cordial, but she didn't care. He was fading from her mind already. And school, with its gossip and social convolutions, was over until fall.

When she got home, Libby reminded her of her doctor's appointment.

"Oh, please, Libby. Let me go to sleep. I can rest now. School's over. I'll get better if I can just stay in bed."

"Nope. Get in the car. This has gone on too long. You can sleep on the way."

She did. She woke up as Libby was pulling into a parking space in front of Dr. Paul's office. Dr. Paul had been her doctor ever since he delivered her one rainy May evening. He'd set her broken arm, put stitches in her chin, taken out her tonsils, made house calls when she'd had the measles, the mumps, and chicken pox, and always told her a joke and gave her a lollipop when he was through.

"What's up, Robin?" Dr. Paul asked as he entered the examining room. She was seated on the examining table in a white paper johnny that tied up the back. "Your grandmother tells me you've been a bit under the weather."

"She worries too much. I've had the flu and I had to

keep going to school because of finals so I couldn't get enough rest to get better. And it's been so hot, it makes me feel dragged out all the time."

He stuck a thermometer in her mouth. "Let's check you over and see what's going on." He took her blood pressure. "That looks fine." He withdrew the thermometer. "Hmmm. Temp's up a bit, but not too bad."

"What is it?"

"One hundred point four. Let's get some blood and urine from you, too. Anything hurt?"

"I'm achy, but mostly I'm just so tired."

"Lie down and let me give you a good going over."

Dr. Paul held up her arms. "Where'd you get these bruises? You been in a fight?"

"Bruises?" she asked, noticing for the first time several dark blotches on the underside of her arms. "I don't know. Doing chores, I guess."

She almost fell asleep while he examined her, and the thought of having to get dressed again nearly made her cry. Her head throbbed and her eyeballs were dry and scratchy.

"What's black and white and has fuzz inside?" he asked, handing her a lollipop.

She'd heard it before, but it always disappointed him when she knew the punch lines, so she shrugged.

"A police car." He laughed and she mustered a smile. "I'll call you Friday with the test results. Now go home and go to bed."

"I can't wait. Talk to you on Friday."

She fell asleep in the car on the way home, lulled by

the hum of the air-conditioning, and for the next two days she slept almost constantly.

Late Friday afternoon she made her way down the back stairs to the kitchen, where Libby was making dinner. Libby stood at the counter slapping chicken parts into beaten egg and then into bread crumbs, scattering egg and crumbs across the counter.

"What did that poor chicken do to make you so mad?" Robin asked, coming up behind her.

Libby dropped a piece of chicken on the floor. "Oh, my stars, you trying to give me apoplexy?" She held her hand over her heart. "I didn't hear you coming."

"Obviously," Robin said, putting a pinch of bread crumbs in her mouth.

"You must be feeling better. Good enough to sneak up on your old grandmother and scare her half to death."

"I am," she said. It wasn't quite true, but she had to start feeling better eventually, and she didn't want Libby to fuss over her anymore.

"High time you ate a decent meal, too. I don't like to see you so thin. How'd you like a glass of milk and some cookies while you wait for dinner?"

"Okay." She would try, for Libby, to eat.

Libby set a glass of milk and a plate of cookies before Robin.

"Now, if I don't get these little old chickens in the pan, we won't be having any dinner. Your daddy wouldn't like that one bit. He comes in from those fields dripping wet and hungry as a bear. Never says a word about how

hard he's working, though." She dropped the chicken parts
into a pan of hot fat. "The most he ever says is 'Hot out
there today,' or something like that. Julie must have felt
like she was talking to herself. Lucky you came along to
answer her back. I always liked a talkative man, myself.
A man who could make a joke, too. That's important.
Goodness knows, life gives you little enough to laugh
at." She turned the chicken pieces. "My Julie could laugh
all right. I never knew a sunnier child. She saw something special in your father, though—that's what I always
told myself. She could have had a lot of different boys,
but she wanted him. And she was happy with him, too.
I'm grateful to him for that. I didn't understand why she
picked him, but I'm grateful she was happy. Then, there's
lots of couples I can't figure out why they're together, so
what do I know? Made a couple of peculiar choices myself, so there you are."

"Boy, Libby, you're sure starved for somebody to talk
to," Robin said. "I ought to give you a parrot for Christmas."

Libby turned from the stove and laughed. "I guess you're
right. I'm a talker, and it's hard on me not to have an
audience." She came over to Robin and hugged her. "I'm
glad you're feeling better. I've got my audience back."

The screen door banged as Will came into the kitchen,
his shirt soaked and stuck to him. "Robin," he said, surprised. "So you finally decided to wake up." He went to
the sink to wash his hands. "Hot out there today."

Libby poked Robin in the ribs with her elbow.

"I'll change my shirt and be right down." He went up

the back stairs, leaving behind a haze of dust that he carried in from the fields.

Libby put the chicken on a platter and filled serving bowls with mashed potatoes and green beans. "There's a chocolate layer cake for dessert, too," she said as she set the dishes on the table.

Will came down the stairs and took his place opposite Robin, with Libby in the middle. Libby bowed her head and held one hand out to Will and one to Robin. They took her hands and then bowed their heads, too. No one spoke for several moments. Then Libby raised her head, picked up the platter of chicken, and offered it to Will.

Libby thought everybody should believe in something. She didn't care what they called it, God, or Fate, or the Wind in the Trees, as long as they paid some recognition to the fact that there was clearly a superior intelligence at work keeping the planets in their orbits, the sun in the sky, and humans and animals reproducing themselves. She also liked to have someone to address her prayers to. "I don't know if praying works," she always said, "but it usually makes me feel better. Maybe that's how it works."

"Did Dr. Paul call?" Robin asked.

"Yes. Yes, he did." Libby passed Robin the chicken. Will stopped chewing and looked at her. "He called while you were out with the cultivator. Did you expect me to run around a thousand acres looking for you? I didn't even know if you were in the corn or the beans."

"Well?" Robin asked.

"Well, uh, he thinks you should have a few more tests."

Will put his fork down. "Why?"

"How should I know? The other ones weren't enough, I guess."

"Enough for what? All she had was the flu. Didn't she?"

"I'm not a doctor. Don't ask me." An unfamiliar vibration in Libby's voice made Robin look at her more closely.

"When's she supposed to have these tests?"

"Monday. As soon as possible, he said. He wants her to go to the hospital in Jefferson and stay a few days—three or four, he said—to make sure she gets all the tests done right."

"Hospital?" Robin asked. Her mother had died in the hospital in Jefferson.

"Bennett's a little town," Libby said defensively. "We don't have the right facilities. Jefferson's only an hour's drive."

Something is changing now, Robin thought. I'm going to remember this conversation for a long time.

"I'll go with her," Will said.

"How can you, Daddy?" Robin asked. "What about the farm? This is a busy time of the year."

"Raymond can watch things. That's what you have a hired man for."

"It's too much for one person now. I can go alone. I can drive myself. It's just for tests."

"Don't be silly," Libby said. "I'll go with her. It'd drive you nuts, Will, sitting around waiting, the way you have to do. I can have Minerva bring you over dinner every night."

Robin stood up. "Don't make it so complicated. Libby can take me, talk to the doctor, and come home. Then she can come back and get me when I'm through. I can talk to you on the phone. So can the doctors. There's no need to disrupt everything, or for one of you to pay money we can't afford for a hotel room and restaurants so you can sit around all day being bored. That's crazy."

"Your grandmother and I will decide," Will said.

Robin went upstairs and lay on her bed. The only reasons she could think of for needing more tests were bad ones.

She remembered when her mother had been in the hospital in Jefferson. Robin had spent hours watching her, waiting for her eyes to open, hoping the efficient doctors and nurses could make that happen. The drunk who had smashed into the truck Julie was driving had escaped with a cut over his right eyebrow; Julie stayed in a coma for eleven days and then died. Robin would never forget how the truck looked: the driver's side crushed beyond repair; the passenger side and the bed, loaded with groceries, medicine for the sick cow, a 94-pound bag of cement, material for a dress for Robin, two rolls of baler twine, and a sack of chicken feed, looking as ordinary as if that day was any regular shopping day.

Returning to that hospital was going to be awful.

Robin spent Saturday in town. She told Libby she was going to visit Marci and look for a robe to wear in the hospital. Instead, she went to the library and looked up her symptoms, which now included the unexplained bruises on her arms and elsewhere. It turned out they could mean a variety of things, from being anemic to having any one of several rare and fatal diseases. She wished she hadn't looked. She wished she still thought her fever and lingering fatigue were results of the flu.

Sunday she went to church with Libby. She didn't go often, though it pleased Libby when she did. Libby had long ago quit urging her, or Will, who never chose to go.

She stood beside Libby and listened to her sing. "Morning has broken, like the first morning. Blackbird has spoken, like the first bird." Libby's clear contralto lifted into the vaulted ceiling and Robin could imagine it sailing past the glowing stained-glass windows and the rotating ceiling fans, squeezing through the joints of the roof, and soaring straight to God's ear.

Reverend Lyon began his sermon. "This morning I have chosen for my topic, 'God Tempers the Wind to the Shorn Lamb.' " He cleared his throat. "We've all had times in our lives when we felt we couldn't take any more; that our sorrows were more than we could bear."

Robin couldn't think of anybody who looked less like his name. He held his Bible in his two little hands in front of his chest and she half expected him to dip down and take a bite from it. If she'd been naming him, he would be Reverend Hamster.

"Our Lord is merciful. He never gives us more than we can bear. *You* may think you have all you can handle, but Our Lord knows us better than we do ourselves. He knows when we can bear more and when we can't. Trust him. Let him decide. Lean on the Lord. Indeed and verily, the wind is tempered to the shorn lamb."

Robin wondered what Reverend Hamster would say about the sheep who froze to death in the winter when they couldn't find shelter from the storms or food under the snow. The wind wasn't tempered to those lambs. She knew what he'd say, though. The same thing Libby would say. "His ways are wondrous strange, and ours not to question."

She glanced across the aisle to where Marci sat twiddling with the narrow white plastic belt on her dress. She bet Marci wouldn't be able to tell her the subject of the sermon five minutes after it was over.

" 'Come to me, all who labor and are heavy laden, and I will give you rest.' He means it. He may test you, yes. Did He not test Job?"

Robin's eyes watered as she yawned, trying not to open her mouth. How long was this going to last? Looking around at the congregation, she spotted Mr. Phillips, her history teacher, sitting with his wife. School rumor was that he had something going with Miss Ziegler, the music teacher. In front of him was Charles Nichols, the president of the bank. He'd been suspected of doing something funny with the bank's assets a few years before, but nothing had ever been proven. In front of him was Maggie Nelson, the town gossip. What did these people learn from being here? What good did going to church do them? Would they be even worse without it? Were they failing their tests or passing them? What about people like Libby who were good even without church? It all became very confusing when she thought about it.

"For He has said, 'I will never fail you nor forsake you.'

Hence, we can confidently say, 'The Lord is my helper, I will not be afraid; what can man do to me?' Hebrews 13:5 and 6. Please rise for the hymn."

Robin sprang to her feet, her hymnal already open to "In the Garden."

At the coffee hour in the church hall after the service, Marci joined Robin, while Libby chatted with some of her friends.

"You don't look any better than the last time I saw you. I thought you were supposed to be getting well."

"I feel better," Robin lied. "When do you start work at the Dairy Queen?"

"Tomorrow. Come on by and I'll give you a free sundae. You could stand some fattening up. I wouldn't mind catching about five pounds of that flu myself. When do you start at the library?"

"Not until next week." Between Ivan, finals, and her illness, she'd almost forgotten about her part-time summer job as library aide.

"You want to do something tomorrow night?" Marci asked.

Robin should have had an answer prepared, but she didn't. After a silence she said, "I can't. Libby and I are going to Jefferson and I don't know what time we'll be back."

"Shopping?"

She hesitated. "Yes."

"I wish I could go with you, but I'll be a working girl by then. Call me when you get back and tell me what you bought. I've got to go now. My mother is giving me her Look."

Robin wandered over to where Libby stood talking to her friend Minerva Hayle. She lingered a bit behind Libby so she wouldn't have to join the conversation, while she puzzled over why she hadn't told Marci the real reason she was going to Jefferson. Was she trying to protect Marci from alarm? Or herself?

Libby said her goodbyes to Minerva and she and Robin walked out to Libby's old Cadillac. "Seems a little cooler today," Libby said, "but my hose are still sticking to my legs. I wish it would rain."

As they drove along the highway toward home, the speedometer needle five miles above the speed limit, Robin asked, "Libby, do you think God really does temper the wind to the shorn lamb? Or does He pay any attention at all?"

"It sure seems like some shorn lambs get a full blast of cold air, doesn't it?" Libby said. "But maybe they're the lambs that can take it."

"But why should they have to?"

"I don't know, doll baby, but I like to think there's a reason for everything, whether I know what it is or not. Maybe the one who suffers the most gets the biggest reward." She paused. "That would be nice."

"How can there be a good reason for some of the awful things that happen? For wars and people starving and things like that?"

"I don't know, honey. That's why I like to think somebody who understands everything better than I do is in charge; that there's a reason I'm too simple to fathom." She adjusted the air-conditioning. "Something I do understand is that you need to put a little meat on your bones. What do you want for supper? I'll make anything you say. Now, what sounds good to you?"

The truth was, nothing sounded good to Robin—she just wasn't hungry. But she said, "How about ham and corn bread."

"Nothing easier," Libby said happily, wheeling the big car smartly into the driveway in front of the farmhouse.

The next morning Libby and Robin were in the car again right after breakfast. It was already hot and the fields along the highway looked parched and glaring, blasted by the sun. The air-conditioning in Libby's car roared.

With each blazing day, Will grew more and more anxious about his crops. When Robin thought of him, she pictured him driving the tractor, turning first to look at the harrow behind him, then to the blank blue of the sky, etching new squint lines around his eyes.

"You got everything you need?" Libby asked. "Toothpaste? Something to read? I don't know why they have to keep you so long. Three days is long enough to do every test ever invented. Probably for nothing, too. Scare a body to death for no good reason. Makes you wonder what goes on in doctors' minds."

So Libby's as afraid as I am, Robin thought.

When they got to the hospital, they spent an unreasonable amount of time filling out forms and going from one office to another before Robin was finally assigned a room and taken to it. There were four beds in the room—one with a curtain drawn around it, one with a sleeping woman in it, and two empty ones. Libby bustled about, unpacking Robin's few things, and then stood by the bed, holding her purse in both hands.

A nurse came in with a lunch tray. She pulled over Robin's bedside stand and put the tray on it. "My name's Virginia," she said. "I bet I could get another tray if you two would like to eat lunch together."

Libby looked at Robin, who nodded.

"Be right back," Virginia said.

When she returned with Libby's lunch, she said, "Robin's first test isn't until three o'clock, so take your time. I'll see you later."

"I can still stay over," Libby said to Robin as they ate their chicken salads. "It'd be nothing to get a hotel room and call Minerva to do for your dad. She wouldn't mind."

"It's okay, Libby, really. I'll be fine and it'll be over before you know it."

After lunch, Libby took up her handbag and kissed Robin. "I'll call you every night," she said, and quickly turned to leave, her eyes bright.

Robin felt very much alone, sitting on her bed. The sleeping woman's lunch remained untouched on her table. No lunch had been brought to the curtained bed. What was she supposed to do now? It was only one-fifteen. She didn't want to put on a nightgown and get in bed—she wanted to feel like a person and not a patient for a while longer. She decided to explore the hospital.

The air had a sharp smell to it that burned her nostrils, and the contrast between the bustling nurses and the immobile sick people made her uncomfortable. Every time she saw someone in a hospital robe shuffling down a hall, she wondered what was wrong with him.

She leafed through magazines in the gift shop, then visited the nursery to watch the newborns. They all looked so raw and unfinished, it was hard to believe they would grow into proper people.

She was surprised to find she couldn't remember which room her mother had been in. It was something she thought she'd never forget, but now all the rooms looked the same.

As she roamed along a corridor on the top floor, she passed a pair of glass doors with the word SOLARIUM on them. She pushed open the doors and went in. The room was long and empty, with many windows, and was furnished with tables, chairs, and lounges. A bank of food and drink machines stood along one wall. The hum of the vending machines and the glare of sunlight filled the room. She found enough change in her pocket to get a drink from one of the machines.

Taking her can, she sat in a chair by the farthest window, looking down on the streets of Jefferson. Outside, all those people were going about their business, never giving a thought to the ones whose worlds had shrunk to the size of a hospital room. She remembered when her mother was here, being astonished that she could still go to school and brush her teeth and watch TV—all the ordinary things that seemed so trivial compared to her mother's struggle. And when her mother died, how surprised she was that the world continued to move along, unimpressed by the catastrophe. Robin had felt like shouting, "Stop everything! How dare you act like nothing has changed!"

She heard footsteps behind her and turned to find a tall blond young man in a hospital bathrobe pushing an IV on a stand. His deep tan made him look too healthy to be dressed the way he was.

"Mind if I sit here?" he asked, indicating the chair next to her. There were many other chairs in the room, and no other people. She frowned, then shook her head.

He sat down and stretched his long legs. "You visiting somebody?"

"No." She didn't want to talk right now; there was too much in her own mind that needed sorting.

"You a patient?"

"Yes. I guess so."

"What does that mean?"

Couldn't he see she wasn't in the mood for company? "I'm here for some tests, that's all."

"Do you think I'm being rude?"

She looked up at him. He was about nineteen and had a square open face and smoky gray eyes. "Yes. You ask a lot of questions. And I'm upset to begin with."

"I know what you mean. I hate hospitals."

"This is the first time I was ever in one. Except to visit."

"I've been in lots of times," he said.

"How come?"

"Why do you think? I've been in the hospital a lot of times because I've been sick a lot."

"Well, excuse *me*," Robin said. "I didn't start this conversation, remember?"

"Look, I'm sorry. I don't know what's the matter with me. Well, actually I do know. It's the chemotherapy, especially the steroids. They mess up my moods. I'm not usually like this. If you want to get up and walk out, I'll understand."

Robin didn't move. "Oh," she said in a small voice. "You have cancer?"

He nodded. "Leukemia."

"I'm scared that's what I have, too," she said softly.

"Oh, God," he said. "I'm sorry. That's what your tests are for?"

"I don't know. I've had this flu that won't go away—that's what everybody keeps calling it, anyway. But I went to the library and looked up my symptoms and they could all mean I have leukemia. Or a few other horrible things. I think my grandmother knows something she's not telling me, but I'm afraid to ask her."

"Everybody's so frightened of cancer," he said thoughtfully. "It's like having a curse put on you. I wonder if they'd have told you if the tests were for something wrong with your eyes. I bet they would have. Weird, isn't it? I'd rather have cancer than be blind or have no arms. I might get cured of cancer. There's no cure for blindness or no arms."

"There's artificial arms," she said, wanting for some reason to reassure him. "You could still function."

"I don't want to just function. I want to be whole. More than whole. Is there a word for being more than whole, better than normal? I've been sick for so long I don't want to be only *better,* I want to be clear on the other side of better. Where nothing can touch me again."

"I hope there is such a place."

"Me, too. How long are you here for?"

"Three or four days. How about you?"

"About the same. I come once a month for a few days. I get zapped with the beetle squeezings, then feel rotten while they watch over me, then go home, then come back and do it all over again."

"Beetle squeezings?" she asked.

"That's what I call my chemotherapy. Whoever invents that stuff always gives it some unpronounceable name so you can never remember what you're taking. And if you should catch on after a while, they change your medication, so you're right back where you started. So I just call it all beetle squeezings. I don't know why they can't give medicine nice catchy names the way they do detergents. Names like Bacteria Blaster, or Extra-Strength Heal, or Mr. Cure. They could use a good PR man."

Robin laughed. "Is that what you want to do?"

"Heck, no. I want to be a microwave-oven repairman. Either that or work for an industrial rubber-supply house."

"Are you serious?"

"Hardly ever. There's so much serious stuff going on all the time, why should I add to the surplus? Besides, it drives my father nuts and anything that can do that to him can't be all bad."

"Sounds like you don't get along with your father."

"Give the lady a cigar. Well, we used to be friends, the Iron Man and me. But not since I got sick. He takes it as a personal affront. Fortunately, he's got enough money to spare no effort at curing me. Hate to tell you this, Dad, but some things are out of even *your* control."

"Are you going to be sorry you're telling me all this?" she asked, surprised at his openness. "You don't know anything about me."

"And never will, so it doesn't matter. The old stranger-on-the-bus syndrome. You can tell somebody like that your most personal business, knowing they'll never do anything about it except go home and say, 'Mabel, I met the oddest person on the bus today. You'll never believe what he told me.' What room are you in?"

"Three-O-six. Why?"

"I want to be sure I avoid that room. We must never meet again. If anybody asks you, tell them you've never heard of me."

"I never have. I don't know your name."

"Fine. Let's keep it that way." He got up. "I'm afraid I have to go toss my lunch. Farewell, my lovely," he said, and wheeled his IV aparatus away with him.

Robin watched him go. "Mabel," she thought, "I met the oddest person in the hospital solarium today." The clock on the wall read almost three o'clock, so she finished her drink, threw the can away, and went back to her room.

Nothing had changed. The curtains were still drawn around the one bed, the second was still empty, and the woman in the third still slept, though her lunch tray was gone.

As she sat on her bed wondering what would happen next, a technician with a metal basket full of glass tubes came into the room.

"You Robin Gregory?" he asked. She nodded, but he checked the plastic band around her wrist anyway. "I'm

Dr. Dracula. I've come for a little sample, heh, heh, heh. It's okay, kid, don't look at me like that. I need some blood from you, that's all. You got a quart to spare? Just let me put this thing around your arm, like that. Now, make a fist. Don't hit me with it, just hold it there. I'm going to stick you a little bit. It shouldn't hurt, but if it does, you can scream. I'll just lose my job, that's all, but go ahead, scream if you have to."

While he was talking, he had already drawn a full syringe of blood and Robin had hardly noticed. "That wasn't so bad, now, was it?" he asked her, untying the rubber tubing around her arm. "I'm sure this'll be delicious. See you later, kid." And he whisked out the door.

As soon as he disappeared, an orderly came in with a wheelchair. "Gregory?" he asked, reaching for her wristband. "X-ray," he said.

"Do I have to go in a wheelchair? There's nothing wrong with me. I can walk."

"Regulations," he said. "Wheelchair."

She obediently sat in the wheelchair and was taken to X-ray by the orderly, who didn't say another word to her. Dr. Dracula's talkativeness had been much more calming.

She waited for half an hour, becoming more and more agitated, before it was her turn. Photographing her from every possible angle took almost an hour, and then she had to sit in the hall waiting for someone to come wheel her back to her room. By then, it was dinnertime.

Her roommate situation remained unchanged. When Virginia brought in her dinner tray, Robin asked what was wrong with the others in her room.

"That lady in the corner's had a stroke. She's in a coma, has been for a couple of weeks. This other lady had her gallbladder out early this morning. It takes a while for the anesthesia to wear off. She'll be more company tomorrow."

Robin pushed rubbery roast beef around in its gummy gravy, ate a bite of mashed potatoes and one of peas, and gave up. She pushed her tray away and reached for the phone to call Libby and her father. Though she had nothing special to tell them, it made her feel better to hear their voices and to know they were waiting for her at home.

After she hung up, she went down the hall for a shower and shampoo. When she came back to her room, the boy from the solarium was sitting beside her bed, his IV stand next to him, reading a farming magazine.

"Hi," she said. "I thought we weren't going to meet again."

"I wondered if you might be lonesome now that visiting hours are over."

"I didn't have any visitors anyway. We live on a farm just outside Bennett, so it's too far to come just for a visit."

"We have a farm, too—over near Moreland. Eleven thousand acres. My father always refers to it as The Property, like it was a plantation. It's got an operating budget that could run Rhode Island, so maybe he's right. You want to go out to the lounge and watch TV?"

"Sure," she said, grateful to escape her inert roommates. "Just let me brush my hair." She took off the towel wrapped around her wet head and brushed out the tangles.

"You have pretty hair."

"Thank you," she said, blushing. Ivan never said anything about the way she looked unless he thought it was sexy. "Are you feeling better?" she asked, wanting to change the subject.

"I'm starting to." He stood up and pushed his IV stand as they walked out to the patients' lounge. "I had the worst of the beetle squeezings yesterday. I'll probably go home tomorrow afternoon, as soon as I feel like I can drive. The first day's always the nastiest. After that, I'm mostly just tired and moody—with an occasional digestive indiscretion."

Robin sat on a plastic-covered couch while the boy switched on the set and twirled the dial from channel to channel. "Oh, my God, oh, my God," he said suddenly. "My favorite movie of all time is coming on! I have to warn you, I permit no talking during this picture. Just at the commercials."

He sat down next to Robin on the couch. "What movie is it?" she asked.

"*Casablanca*. With you-know-who."

"Who? I've never seen it."

"What! You've never seen *Casablanca*? I believe that's a felony. At least a misdemeanor. Humphrey Bogart, of course, that's who's in it. And Ingrid Bergman, the most delectable woman ever born. She takes my breath away. Now pay attention to this great beginning. The narrator has a voice that makes the floor vibrate."

The beginning of the movie seemed like any old-fashioned black-and-white movie to Robin. She couldn't see what was so special about it. Ingrid Bergman *was* gorgeous, though.

At the first commercial he turned to her. "Tell me the truth, now. Don't you see a strong resemblance between me and Humphrey Bogart?"

"Well, honestly, I can't say that I do. He's a little dark guy and you're tall and fair. He's got some kind of speech impediment and he smokes and wears a tuxedo. You're in pajamas, eating linty licorice from your bathrobe pocket."

"Actually, the resemblance is more to his character, Rick, than to him. Don't tell me you've missed my suaveness, my savoir-faire, my coolth, stuff like that."

Robin laughed. "Sure, I spotted your coolth right away."

"I knew it. You want some licorice?"

"No, thanks. It's too fuzzy."

"Improves the taste," he said, popping a piece into his mouth.

The boy knew most of the movie by heart and could recite lines with the characters for minutes at a time. "This is the only movie I own," he told her. "I must have played it a hundred times on our VCR."

"Aren't you tired of it?" she asked. "I don't think I could see any movie a hundred times."

"Watch your mouth! Get tired of *Casablanca*? A man who's tired of *Casablanca* is tired of life! Now, the greatest scene is in this next section, where he's reading the letter at the station and it rains on the words and makes them smear. It's genius."

"Sounds kind of corny to me."

He looked at her in shock, then smiled sadly. "Clearly you are a bumpkin. Take my word for it, it's genius. Watch."

At the end of the movie, when Rick makes Ilsa get on the plane leaving Casablanca with Victor Laszlow, Robin got tears in her eyes and had to wipe them with her bathrobe sleeve.

The boy patted her hand. "I know. It gets to me every time, too. What nobility. Well, what do you think? Fantastic, right?"

"I don't know—maybe I need to see it a few more times. It seemed kind of melodramatic."

He looked aghast.

"The ending was good, though. It was pretty romantic."

"The whole movie is romantic!" He shook his head. "Don't worry, you can become educated."

A nurse appeared at the door of the lounge. "Hey, what are you two doing here? You should be in bed. This is a hospital, not a nightclub."

"No chance of mistaking it for a nightclub, Miss Nightingale," he said. "Come along, my dear." He stood up and held his hand out to Robin. "You've just had a serious emotional experience, even if you're too much of a hayseed to know it, and it does take its toll. You have to let at least two weeks go by between viewings. Longer than that for beginners."

He walked her to her room. "Good night, Gregory, Robin. Thanks for a wonderful evening."

"How did you know my name?" she asked.

"I can read upside down."

She glanced down at the name band around her wrist. Quickly she looked for the one on his wrist, but he clapped his hand over it. "Ha! Too fast for you. I prefer to remain a mystery. See you tomorrow." He bent and kissed her on the cheek, then wheeled his IV stand off down the hall to the elevator, waving as he went.

The lady who'd had the gallbladder surgery was turned on her other side; otherwise, nothing in the room had changed.

Robin was exhausted and grateful to get to bed. She was grateful, too, for the way the boy had been able to keep her mind off the reason she was in the hospital. She wondered if he had done it on purpose. He would know, if anyone would, how anxious she felt. She realized, as she sank into sleep, that she had had a better time with him, sitting on a cheap plastic couch in her bathrobe watching a movie so old everyone in it was dead, than she had ever had with Ivan, whatever they had done.

The next day was a busy one, with more going from one lab or special machine to another, more waiting, and more tests, including a bone-marrow biopsy, which was the most painful ordeal of her life.

About four o'clock Robin was brought back to her room in a wheelchair, pale and limp with fatigue and fear, her hospital gown crumpled and stained, her hair tangled around her face, and found the boy, dressed in jeans and a red polo shirt, waiting for her. She wasn't expecting the thump her heart gave when she saw him.

"Hi," she said, moving shakily from the wheelchair to her bed.

"Hi, Gregory, Robin. You've been gone quite a while. Have they been giving you a bad time?"

"Have you ever had a bone-marrow test?"

"I thought of warning you, but I figured you were already scared enough."

She eased her head down onto the pillow. "Are you going home now?" She glanced at his wrist, but the plastic band was gone.

"Yes, but I didn't want to leave until I'd told you goodbye. I'm glad you were here. You made it easier."

"Thanks. You did for me, too."

He stuck his hands in his back pockets. "Strangers on a bus. Ships that pass in the night. All that jazz. I hope everything's okay with your tests."

She nodded. "Yeah. Me, too. Well, goodbye. Good luck."

"Thanks." He stood looking at her. "Well, I guess I better go." He put his hands on the pillow, bracketing her face, and kissed her forehead. "I left you a present. It's under your pillow." He turned and left the room.

Gingerly she propped herself up enough to slide her hand under the pillow and pulled out a plastic wristband snipped in the middle. She turned it so she could read the name: WINN, RICHARD.

After not eating dinner again, Robin talked to Libby and Will, avoiding mention of the bone-marrow test. She told them Dr. Schwartz had been in to see her before dinner and said there would be only one more test the next morning and then she could go home. He would be able to talk to Libby about the test results when she came to get Robin.

"Oh, that's wonderful, honey plum. What time should I come?"

"He said I'll be through by eleven and he can see us at noon. Is that okay?"

"You bet! I'll see you tomorrow."

"Good night, Libby. Good night, Daddy."

"Good night, Robin. Hurry home," her father said.

After the phone call, she lay in bed, her mind blunt, unable even to read. She wanted tomorrow and the conference with Dr. Schwartz to come so the suspense would be over. But she also wished it would never come. What if the news was bad? Then what would she do?

She wished Winn, Richard were there to talk to. The lady with the gallbladder surgery was too groggy to be any company. Her husband had been there, sitting by her bed for a couple of hours, but she kept falling asleep, and now visiting hours were over and he was gone. The nurses came in once in a while to turn the lady in the coma, or to change her IV. Otherwise, it was dim and quiet in the room, and the sounds from the corridor were muted as the evening nursing shift settled into the less hectic nighttime routine.

Robin jumped when the phone by her bed rang. "Hello?"

"Hi, Gregory, Robin. Guess who?"

"Winn, Richard?"

"Call me Rick. As in *Casablanca*. Nobody but my mother calls me Richard. What are you doing?"

"Counting sheep. I'm up to twelve thousand and thirty-eight. What are you doing?"

"Thinking about you. When do you get your test results?"

"Tomorrow at noon."

"Are you nervous? Forget it. Dumb question. You'd be crazy not to be nervous. Would you mind letting me know what they are? I could call you at home tomorrow night."

She gladly gave him her phone number. "How do you feel?"

"Good. I feel good. Having somebody to talk to helps."

"You must have people you can talk to."

"I've always been kind of a loner. I mean, people seem to like me, but I'm choosy about who I like back. Since I've been sick I'm even choosier. Some people are *sooo* sympathetic they make you want to barf. And I do enough of that with the chemotherapy. Some people are scared of you, as if cancer were contagious. Hardly anybody treats you normally. Even my mother—she used to be a regular mother—you know, overprotecting you when you want to be independent and ignoring you when you want attention, but now she's too nice to me. And she does a lot of crying. And you know about my father. I'm glad you were there, Gregory, Robin."

"I'm glad you were there, too. I'd be a wreck by now if you hadn't been."

"Okay, G.R. I'll talk to you tomorrow night. I hope the news is all good."

"Thanks, Rick. Good night."

She hung up the phone, turned off her light, and slid down in bed, thinking about the farm: the scent of the lilacs by the front porch that drifted up to her open window on damp spring nights; the hot buzz of insects in the fields at midday in summer; the sound of the combine starting up early in the morning during harvest while she still lay half asleep; the winter-morning sounds of Libby in the kitchen while Robin dressed for school, coffee and bacon smells winding up the stairs: all the taken-for-granted parts of her life seemed somehow exotic in the antiseptic, proscribed routine of the hospital. At that moment it seemed Marci was right—there was no better place to be than Bennett.

The next morning she had a liver scan and then went back to her room to pack and wait for Libby, who arrived even before eleven. Libby rushed into the room, swept Robin into an enormous hug, and kissed her on both cheeks.

"Oh, have I missed you! I wished I had that parrot already! How you doing, honey plum? You want some lunch before we see the doctor, or after? You all packed and ready to go home? We're sure ready to have you back. Even the chickens miss you. I guess I don't feed them like you do. How do you feel?"

"Slow down!" Robin said. "I can't remember all the questions! I'm not hungry enough for lunch now. Let's wait until after. Yes, I'm all packed. I feel okay. Is that all of them?"

"Make fun of me all you want," Libby said, hugging her again. "I don't care. I'm so glad to see you."

"Something interesting happened, too."

"Interesting? What do you mean?"

"I met a boy. A really nice, funny boy."

Libby raised her eyebrows. "See? All you have to do is leave Bennett for a day! Is he a patient?"

"He's gone now. He was just here for . . . for treatment."

"Treatment? Treatment for what?"

Robin took a deep breath, then rushed on. "For leukemia. But he was great, Libby—easy to talk to and nice and full of ideas. He called me last night. And he's going to call me at home tonight."

"Well, well, well," Libby said with effort. "He sounds special. What's his name? Where's he from?"

"His name's Rick Winn. He's from around Moreland."

"Winn? His dad wouldn't be Tad Winn, would he? The Winns have got a great big farm over that way, about the only one making any real money from farming in the whole county. I hear he runs that place like a dictator."

"That sounds like the way Rick described him."

"Pretty fancy company you're keeping. Well, come on. Let's go throw your stuff in the car and have a cup of tea before we see the doctor."

At twelve o'clock Libby and Robin were waiting outside Dr. Schwartz's office. The nurse showed them in and he rose from behind his desk to shake hands with Libby.

"Hi, Robin, Mrs. Clayton. Please sit down." He folded his hands on his desk and waited until they were settled. "We've been very thorough in our testing with Robin," he said quietly. "We prefer to err on the side of caution— it avoids mistakes with diagnoses." He hesitated. "I wish we'd made a mistake in this case. All indications are that Robin has acute lymphocytic leukemia."

Robin saw Dr. Schwartz's mouth moving and heard a

buzz of sound, but only three words rang in her head: *acute lymphocytic leukemia.* She turned to look at Libby.

Libby's lips were clenched together and her hands clasped each other so tightly in her lap that her knuckles were white.

Robin looked back at the doctor, whose face was grave and kind. Gradually his words began to make sense again. ". . . an aggressive course of therapy, we can hope for good results. I can't make any promises or predictions, but with a combination of radiation and chemotherapy we have fairly good luck with inducing remissions. I know this is a shock—do you have any questions you'd like to ask me now?"

Robin and Libby simply looked at him. Then Libby said in a small voice, "Is there any chance there's been a mistake? Maybe someone read the tests wrong. Maybe these are someone else's tests."

Dr. Schwartz shook his head. "I wish there was a chance of that, but no. We're very careful in a case like this. These are Robin's tests and there's no doubt about the accuracy of the diagnosis. I'm sorry." Libby and Robin sat, stunned and silent. "I want you to call me tomorrow. I'm sure by then you'll have thought of some questions you'll want to ask. And I'll be able to tell you about Robin's course of therapy. I'll have the nurse make an appointment time for you to call. We'll do our very best for Robin, and the picture is far from bleak."

He stood, and when he did, Libby and Robin did, too. He held out his hand and they each solemnly shook it before he ushered them into the waiting room, where he instructed the nurse to make them a phone appointment.

Libby and Robin went out into the hall and stood waiting for the elevator. As they entered it, Robin took Libby's hand and clung to it as if they were taking a dangerous trip.

They held hands as they walked across the parking lot to the car, and Libby was the first to speak when they reached it. Her voice was breathy, as though she'd been punched in the stomach. "Lunch. I forgot all about lunch. Are you hungry?"

"No. I just want to go home. I want to get away from here."

"So do I," Libby said, unlocking the car doors.

She guided the car onto the highway and pressed her foot to the accelerator so that they leapt forward, well over the speed limit, toward the boiling of black clouds on the horizon. The sky darkened by the minute as they sped toward Bennett, and the trees by the roadside bent in the wind.

"Looks like we're in for a good storm," Libby said. "Lord knows we could use some rain, but I hope it holds off until we get home. I don't like the idea of driving in it, not the way I feel right now."

A streak of lightning cut the air just as they pulled into the driveway in front of the farmhouse. A blast of thunder broke over their heads and the first fat warm drops of rain spattered onto the dusty yard. They hurried to bring Robin's suitcase from the trunk of the car, but by the time they got to the front door, they were drenched. Will flung the door open and pulled Robin inside, hugging her to him, wet as she was.

Robin burst into tears.

Will looked over her head to Libby. "She's so glad to be home," Libby said. "I'll take this suitcase upstairs. Be back in a minute."

Will fetched a towel from the downstairs bathroom and draped it around Robin's shoulders. "You had lunch? I waited on mine just in case."

Robin wiped her wet face with the towel. "No. We wanted to wait until we got home." They walked down the hall to the kitchen, Will's arm around her.

"I was going to warm up the leftover stew from last night. I can do that while you get into something dry."

"Okay." Upstairs, she put on her oldest, softest jeans and a T-shirt and tried to pretend she had just spent the night at Marci's, but it was no good.

She returned to the kitchen and was stirring the stew when she heard Libby's house shoes, changed from her "town shoes," coming down the back stairs. "Good," Libby said as she came into the kitchen. "You started lunch."

The three of them moved about the kitchen, in silence except for the pouring rain, warming the stew, laying the table, putting out fruit and bread and butter, pouring milk. Finally they sat down together and Libby held her hands out to Will and Robin. She kept her head down and her eyes closed longer than she usually did.

Robin dipped her spoon into the stew but couldn't bring it to her lips. She was afraid she was going to be sick.

Will took a bite of the stew. "It got better with sitting." He looked at Robin and then at Libby. "Well?"

"You must be wondering about my tests," Robin said.

He nodded, his face wary.

Libby cleared her throat. "Dr. Schwartz seems like a very good doctor. Dr. Paul recommends him highly. Says he's a real expert. Really knows what he's doing."

"Expert in what?" Will asked.

"Oh," Libby said. "He's an expert in, uh, diseases of the blood. That's his specialty. You should see his office. One whole wall covered with diplomas and certificates and I don't know what-all. Don't know how he's had time to do any doctoring, what with spending all that time in school."

"What's wrong with Robin?" Will asked.

"Well, he did a lot of tests. Every test you could think of. He said he didn't want to make any mistakes. Wanted to be sure. Nothing worse than making a mistake . . ."

"He says I have acute lymphocytic leukemia," Robin interrupted.

"Oh, God," Will said, and dropped his spoon on the table. He ran his hand through his hair. "Oh, God." He stood up, pushing back his chair so suddenly it fell over. He looked around in a dazed way, as if trying to remember where he was. "Oh, God." He walked out the back door into the rain.

Libby jumped up and ran to the door. "Will! You come back here! You'll catch your dea . . . you'll catch cold!"

He kept walking through the downpour to the barn and disappeared inside.

Libby sat down at the table again. "He used to do that when Julie was sick, remember?" she said. "Go out to the barn at all hours and just stay there. I went after him once when he'd been gone a good long time, and found him standing in the stall with Elsie. Had his arms around that cow's neck and his head down on her, crying. Poor man. Had no other friend to go to."

"That's the worst thing I've ever had to do in my life," Robin said.

Libby stood up and put her arms around Robin from behind. "Doll baby, the hardest thing in the whole world, and I mean there is *nothing* harder, is watching somebody you love hurt. Especially when there's nothing you can do about it. And there usually isn't, not for the real bad hurts." She rested her cheek on top of Robin's head for a minute. "Well, come on, let's get these dishes cleaned up." She began gathering the still-full plates.

"I think I'd like to go upstairs for a while," Robin said.

In her room she had to turn a light on, it was so dark from the storm. The window was open and the curtains, white eyelet ones her mother had made, blew and flapped. Robin shut the window and mopped rain from the windowsill with a towel from the bathroom. She leaned her forehead against the cool glass and, looking at the dark puddles growing in the barnyard, thought of her father with Elsie.

Robin unpacked her suitcase, then turned off the light and lay on her bed listening to the rain. What of her dreams now? What of the future she had always known awaited her outside Bennett?

"It's not fair!" she said into her pillow. "It's not fair! I haven't done anything to deserve this. I know lots of people who've been worse than I have. I don't even drink soft drinks! It's not *fair!*"

There was no answer but the sound of the rain soaking into the thirsty fields. After a time she got up, washed her face, and went downstairs to the kitchen, where Libby was sitting at the table pretending to read the paper.

"I always know where to find you," Robin said.

"That's the truth," Libby answered. "This has always been my favorite room in the house. It's got the best view I know of."

Robin looked out the window. "Has Daddy come back yet?"

"No. But it'll be suppertime soon and I'm sure he'll come in by then. And after supper we'll need to talk so we can be ready for our phone call with Dr. Schwartz tomorrow." She put the paper down and held her arms out to Robin. "I know you must be scared." Robin came into her arms and sat on her lap, the way she hadn't done since she was a little girl. Libby held her, rocking gently back and forth.

As they sat that way, the back door opened and Will came in, expressionless. Robin went to him and put her arms around him. He hugged her, lowering his face into her hair.

After a moment, Libby stood up. "Go wash your hands, Will," she said, "and we'll have some supper."

After the supper dishes had been cleared, the three of them sat down again and thought of questions to ask Dr. Schwartz. Libby wrote them carefully on sheets of tablet paper, while Will automatically tied knot after intricate knot in a length of knitting yarn. They had gotten to the point where they couldn't think of any more when the telephone rang.

"I'll get it," Robin said, and walked down the hall to

the parlor. The storm was almost over, the rain coming in little fits and blusters. The heavy clouds were moving off to the horizon, where they were back-lit with pink and gold from the setting sun.

"Hello?"

"Is this Gregory, Robin?"

"Rick! I'd forgotten you were going to call."

"That's wonderful for my ego. I imagined you waiting breathlessly all day, counting the minutes."

"I'm sorry. I've had a few other things on my mind."

"Your tests?"

"Yes."

"Bad news?"

She told him.

He was quiet for a heartbeat. "Same as me."

"How long have you had it?" She had to ask.

"Two years."

"My mother died three years ago and I thought about death then, but not about dying, not about *me* dying."

"Yeah, it's scary," he said softly. "But there are worse things than dying. Throwing up every fifteen minutes for sixty hours is worse than dying. I did that once with some beetle squeezings they were trying out on me. I hope to God I never have to do that again. Then my hair fell out. But it grew back."

Robin pushed her fingers through her hair.

"It doesn't happen to everybody, though," he said. "Maybe you'll be lucky."

"I'm not feeling too lucky right now."

"You could look on it as a character-building experience."

"Please."

"I'm sorry. That's something my father might say. Look, Robin, I'd like to come see you. I know it's a long drive, but it's summer and I don't have anything else going on. My mother won't let me do much except take the pigs for a walk and sit in the sun."

"I'd like to see you. I want my family to meet you, too—to know that I'm not necessarily doomed."

"We're all doomed, G.R. It's just a question of time. Would you like to hear my quote of the week?"

"What's a quote of the week?"

"Well, I read a lot, since I have a lot of time, and I try to find something every week that I can mull over. This week the quote is from Nathaniel Hawthorne." He paused. " 'We sometimes congratulate ourselves at the moment of waking from a troubled dream: It may be so the moment after death.' How do you like that?"

"I'm not sure. I'll have to think about it."

"That's the idea. When can I come see you?"

"How about this weekend? Saturday?"

"Great. How about if I come for breakfast and stay for dinner. Or do you think that would be overdoing it?"

She smiled. "I think that would be fine, if you really want to."

"I really want to."

She gave him directions to the farm. "See you Saturday."

After she hung up, she sat on the couch in the dark, wishing Saturday was closer.

The phone rang again.

"Hello?"

"Hey, I thought you were going to call me when you got back from Jefferson."

"Hi, Marci. Sorry. I've just been . . . busy, I guess."

"Well, what did you buy? Anything good?"

"No. I . . . I couldn't find anything I liked."

"You're kidding! I bet I could have. Jefferson looks like Paris to me next to Bennett. Nothing but jeans and flowered housedresses here, for goodness' sakes. Are you okay? You sound funny."

"You know rainy days always make me blue." She couldn't think of anything to say to Marci. Rick was right. Knowing she had cancer removed her from her old life. Things like shopping seemed irrelevant.

"Well, I've got something that'll cheer you up. A bunch of us are going out to the Pavilion to dance Saturday night. Come with us. You can hunt for Prince Charming."

"I don't know, Marci. Let me think about it."

"You afraid of seeing Ivan?"

"It's not that. I might have something else to do."

"Yeah? What?"

"I, uh, might have some company."

"Who? What's the matter with you? This is like pulling teeth."

"I'll tell you about it later." If she mentioned Rick, she'd have to tell Marci where she met him and why, and she wasn't ready to do that yet. "And yes, you're right, I don't want to run into Ivan." She forced herself to steer the conversation in Marci's direction. "Especially if he's with another girl."

"Oh, Robin, it would be a perfect chance for you to show him how little he meant to you. You could ignore him and dance with other guys and everybody would see what a good time you were having without him." Marci comfortably settled into a monologue weighing the advantages of Robin's going to the Pavilion Saturday night, while Robin lay on the sofa only half listening. "I wish I could do something with you Saturday afternoon," Marci finally changed the subject, "but it's my little brother's birthday and I have to help my mom with the party. She's paying me to do it, too. She said she wished there was somebody to pay *her* to spend the afternoon breaking up fights and washing frosting off the dog."

"That's okay, Marci. We've got all summer. I'll talk to you later." She hung up, then returned to the kitchen, but Will and Libby had gone upstairs. The lights were off and the sound of the dishwasher filled the dark room.

By Friday, Dr. Schwartz had mapped out a schedule of treatment for Robin. It was to be the same as Rick's: three days in the hospital once a month for six months. She was to begin the next week.

Libby had been surprised when Robin told her Rick was coming for breakfast. "Breakfast? That's an odd date. Why doesn't he come for lunch? Or dinner?"

"He is. Both. He's going to stay all day."

"Well. I guess he must want to see you pretty bad."

"Anything wrong with that?"

"Did I say there was anything wrong with it? If he wants breakfast, I'll show him some breakfast. Maybe I'll make some of my sourdough flapjacks. I haven't made them in a while. Or some corn dodgers. Or both. As I

recall, teenage boys eat like every meal was their last one."
She put her hand over her mouth. "I didn't mean that."
    "I know you didn't. It's just an expression."
    "That's right. What time's he coming?"
    "Early, I hope."

Saturday, Robin was up at dawn and had fed the chickens and milked Elsie even before Libby came downstairs. Will was out even earlier than Robin, mending fences, but promised to be back for lunch. He admitted to being curious about this boy who was driving all the way from Moreland to see his daughter.
    Sitting at the kitchen table, Robin heard a car in the gravel drive. She jumped up, then made herself sit down again, glancing sideways at Libby where she stood by the old black six-burner stove.
    Robin grinned, embarrassed. "I guess that's him."
    "Thank goodness," Libby said. "You're so jumpy you're sending off sparks."
    Robin smoothed her hair, tucked in her shirt more tightly, and ran her damp palms down the sides of her jeans. Taking a deep breath, she started toward the front door just as the bell rang.
    He looked even better than she remembered. She'd forgotten how tall he was, and how gray his eyes were.
    "Hi," Rick said, smiling, one hand behind his back. "Beautiful morning. I'm starving."
    "Hi. What's behind your back?"
    "Nothing you need to worry about."
    She led him to the kitchen. "Rick, this is my grandmother, Libby Clayton. Libby, Rick Winn."

"Hello there, Rick. Are you ready for some breakfast?"

"I could handle some," he said, and brought from behind him a bunch of pink rosebuds wrapped in cellophane and tied with a pink ribbon. "These are for you. Thank you for letting me come and interfere with your Saturday."

"Well," Libby said, momentarily too astonished to take the flowers. "It's not *my* Saturday you're interfering with. It's Robin's, and I don't think it's bothering *her*. But I'll take the flowers anyway. Thank you. Now sit down. I'll have some breakfast for us as soon as I put these pretties in water."

Rick sat at the table while Libby and Robin bustled around the kitchen, readying a breakfast that had been planned the night before and almost completely executed well before Rick showed up.

Libby put a plate of sourdough pancakes in front of him and Rick closed his eyes, inhaling the fragrance blissfully. "If there's a better smell in the world, I can't think of it right now." He waited for Libby and Robin to sit down, then put gobs of butter between the pancakes and drowned the whole pile in maple syrup. Cutting a chunk with his fork, he poked it into his mouth. "Tastes even better than it smells."

Libby laughed, pleased. "I like to see a body with a good appetite. I was afraid you might not be able to eat because . . . oh, there I go!" She slapped her hand on the table, rattling the dishes.

"That's okay," Rick said. "Today I feel fine and I'll eat anything that doesn't eat me first. Not every day is that good, though, so on the good days I go all-out."

"Sound advice for anybody," Libby said, getting up for the coffee pot. "It's a beautiful day, and a mite cooler since that lovely storm. What are you two up to?" She poured each of them more coffee.

Rick looked at Robin.

"I thought I'd show him around the farm this morning and then after lunch we could go in to Bennett."

Robin figured it couldn't hurt for her to be seen in town with another boy. It would be especially nice if Ivan saw her. She needed that loose end tied up.

When they finished breakfast, Libby shooed them from the kitchen. "Go on, get out of here. Go enjoy the day. Come back about twelve-thirty and we'll have some lunch."

"I'm looking forward to it," Rick said as he and Robin went out the back door.

"You don't *have* to stay out until lunch," Libby said, remembering. "If you get tired, come on back and have a rest."

Robin led Rick across the dusty barnyard. No matter how much it rained, the barnyard dust seemed to regenerate itself within hours, and it was impossible in the summer to be outside for very long without acquiring a coating on your clothes, skin, and even tongue.

"You sure charmed Libby," Robin said.

"Shucks," he said, digging his toe in the dirt. "I just can't seem to help it."

"And roses!"

"Why not? Every day's a celebration, as far as I'm concerned."

"Celebration? So far, I've just been scared and angry."

He nodded. "It goes away—some of the time, anyhow. The anger's been harder on me than the fear."

They went into the dim, hazy cool of the barn. "I kept Elsie in so you could see her. We can take her out to pasture now." Dust motes swam in streaks of sunlight and the only sound was the small crackle of hay under their feet as they threaded their way through a maze of tools, buckets, containers of seed and chicken feed and pesticides, coils of rope, and dismantled pieces of farm equipment.

"Here's my Elsie," Robin said when they reached Elsie's stall. She put her arms around the cow's neck. "Isn't she sweet?" Elsie turned her head and rolled her huge eyes in Robin's direction, chewing uninterruptedly.

"Yeah, she's great. Not my type, though."

Robin patted Elsie on the side. "Come on, sweetie. You can go out now. Come on." She guided the cow out the back of the barn, across a strip of dirt, to a gate that opened into a green pasture. When Elsie had gone through the gate, Robin latched it. "This probably doesn't look like much to you. Your place is so much bigger."

They walked to the side yard, where the chickens scratched in the dust. "It's so big it's hardly real," he said. "It's all computerized and mechanized and credit-balanced. We don't even have any animals except hogs. That's because they're cheaper and faster to market than cattle, and they can eat the feed corn we grow. They sure don't have names."

Robin pointed to her chickens. "Well, here even the chickens have names. This is Sleepy, and that's Dopey, that's Sneezy, that's Happy, that's Grumpy, that's Bashful, and the rooster is Doc. They're not economical—neither is Elsie—but my mother thought a farm should have a cow and some chickens, so I keep them."

Rick waved to the chickens, who stopped pecking long enough to stare at him with the angry look that is a chicken's only expression. "She must have been a city girl. They all think farms are like storybooks, full of cute animals."

Robin smiled. "She was. She came to Bennett to teach school. And met my father."

"And had you," he said. "Let's walk through the fields."

The soybean plants were still small and the rows between them were soft and loamy from the rain. As Rick and Robin walked down the rows, their feet left deep footprints and released a rich, earthy smell.

When Robin reached to pull a weed from between the plants, conditioned as almost every farm teenager was by long hours of "walking the beans" in the summertime, Rick stopped her hand. "Don't. That's milkweed."

"So? It's a weed, isn't it?"

"Monarch butterflies lay their eggs in milkweed," he said.

She withdrew her hand and they walked on.

"What you were saying about the anger going away," Robin said. "I can't imagine that it will. I'm angry at everybody who's going to live longer than I am. I'm angry that I have to go through this and be scared and sick and ugly. I'm angry at my body. We've always been friends—I thought I could trust it, and look what it's done to me. It isn't fair."

"You might as well forget about fair. Nothing's fair.

Think of the punishments you didn't get for things you should have. Think of the good deeds you did that went unrewarded. This is the same kind of thing, just on a bigger scale. As far as being mad at everybody who's going to live longer than you are, no matter how long you live, *somebody's* going to live longer. That's true even when you don't have leukemia."

She squinted up at him, the sun in her eyes. "What are you most angry about?"

"Different things than you are. I want to be in college now, but I can't keep up with my treatments and manage school, too. I want to live away from home, but I can't do that either. This is the time when I'm supposed to be going off on my own and finding out about life, and I'm trapped, and it enrages me. I'm angry that this has made my mother so sad and has driven my father away from me. But the stuff you're mad about, the unfairness, I'm mostly over that. I remember it, though, and it's bad." He paused. "Hey, I even feel friends with my body again. It's doing the best it can. Why not think about the part of you that's *not* your body. Who is that? Even if your body is sick—what about that other you? Is that still there?"

"You've spent a lot of time thinking about this, haven't you?"

"I didn't have much choice. My mother made me go to a shrink when I first got sick, but he was so afraid of talking about dying he scared me more. Nobody knows what it feels like except somebody who's there. If you ever feel the need of a shrink, you can come lie down on my couch any time."

She glanced up and he smiled innocently at her.

"It's all I can think about. Every time I do something, I wonder how many more times I'll get to do it. It's like in a horror movie; when you're watching the nice scenes, you know they're not going to last, that something terrible is going to happen without any warning and there's nothing you can do about it."

"All I can tell you, G.R., is that the emergency mentality doesn't last forever. Sooner or later, you have to make a molehill out of that mountain or you'll drive yourself nuts. What good is being alive if you're nuts? One day at a time, that's all you can worry about."

Robin could feel herself relaxing under the flow of his words.

"I don't mean to suggest you can forget you're sick," Rick said. "Oh, you do for hours at a time, sometimes, depending on what you're doing. But it's always there, like a shadow. You just get used to it."

"I need to rest a minute," Robin said, stopping in the shade of a red oak that formed part of the shelter belt at the western edge of the field.

As they sat with their backs against the big tree, Rick took Robin's hand and held it, stroking it with his thumb. "This is nice." He sighed. "I like to see trees in the fields. My father took all our trees out a long time ago. It's easier for the big equipment to go straight down long rows; sixteen-row disc-tillers don't turn easily, and time is money. When I mention trees as a soil-conservation measure he tells me I don't know the first thing about economical farming."

"We've always had trees here—since my great-grandfather. Daddy says nobody's making dirt anymore and we have to save what we have."

"Am I going to get to meet your father?"

"At lunch. We should head back pretty soon."

"Not yet. This is too nice—the best place in the world to be just now."

He was right. Why was she in any hurry? What was so important that she couldn't continue to enjoy this peace? She leaned her head back against the trunk of the tree.

The sun filtering through the leaves of the oak tree sent little gold balls bursting and spinning off into the darkness of her closed eyes. She watched them whirl and spin.

"Hey, G.R., you awake?"

She opened her eyes and saw Rick's face looking into hers. "I . . . I must have dozed for a minute. I felt so relaxed I guess I . . ."

"Another blow to my ego. Take a girl for a walk and the minute I let her sit down she falls asleep. Tell me, am I using the right mouthwash?"

She laughed. "You're just so comfortable to be with."

"Comfortable? What about fascinating? Romantic? Mysterious? What about dashing? Exciting? Irresistible?"

"Oh, well, you're all those other things too, of course," she said, standing up and brushing off the back of her jeans.

"Stop," he said, getting up, too. "You're embarrassing me." He put his hands on her shoulders. "Robin, I . . ."

Suddenly a horn tooted and she heard her father's tractor coming toward them, towing a wagon full of fence-mending equipment.

"Want a ride?" Will called.

Robin waved. "Sure, Daddy."

The tractor stopped and Robin and Rick climbed on. "Daddy, this is Rick Winn. Rick, my dad."

Rick and Will shook hands and Will put the tractor in gear again. "Very nice place you have here, sir."

"Nothing like yours," Will said.

"Big isn't everything," Rick answered. "And how you do it matters most of all."

Will guided the tractor into the barnyard. "Well, I like what I do. Don't know how many people can say that."

Coming through the kitchen door, Rick asked, "What smells so good?"

"It's apple pie," Libby told him. "But that's for dinner. Just wanted to make sure you'd come back for it."

"Don't worry. I'm convinced."

"Go wash up now, all of you," Libby said. "Lunch is on the table."

When they were seated, Libby bowed her head and held out her hands. Rick looked uncertainly at Robin but took her hand and Will's and bowed his head, too.

As the dishes were being passed, Rick turned to Will. "Have you ever given any thought to organic farming?" he asked him.

"You mean without chemical fertilizers, pesticides, and herbicides?"

Rick nodded.

"No. I'm not a big operation—only two hundred and forty acres owned and about eight hundred leased—I can't afford to take any chances on decreasing my yield."

"I subscribe to this magazine, *The New Farm,* and every issue has farmers telling how they cut out the chemicals and haven't had any trouble with productivity." Rick scooped up a second helping of applesauce.

"I've heard about that, but I don't think we can go

back to farming the way we did in the thirties. This is a new time, and requires modern methods. You've got to feed the soil, kill the insects and the weeds to protect your crops."

"You can do it without chemicals, though."

"I just don't believe it," Will said. "I've seen how our productivity has leaped over the years by using chemicals."

Libby put a spoonful of applesauce on Robin's plate as Robin said, "I don't want any more."

"It's good for you," Libby said.

Rick turned to them, but he hardly seemed to see them. "Do you know that insects and plant diseases are becoming immune to chemicals? There are four hundred and twenty-eight arthropods, thirty-six weeds, and ninety plant diseases that are resistant to pesticides now."

"Is that so? Well, they still seem to be working for me. Tell me, does your father use chemicals?"

"Yes, sir, he does."

Will nodded pointedly and drained his glass of iced tea.

Robin was astounded. She had never heard her father talk at such length with a stranger.

Libby passed a bowl to Rick. "Have some of these tomatoes. They're from my garden. *I* don't use chemicals."

After Will returned to his fence-mending, Robin and Rick helped Libby clear the table and then left for Bennett.

"I didn't know you were so interested in farming," Robin said, turning the Honda onto the highway.

"I'm interested in alternative farming. My father says I

don't know what I'm talking about. He's right; my knowledge is all from books. But I *know* it works. Think about it. You can easily spend a hundred dollars an acre on fertilizer. Easily. With a farm the size of yours, that's about a hundred thousand dollars. I bet your father could think of something he'd rather do with that money. Do you know that sixty-two percent of the pesticides in use today have never been tested for cancer-causing potential?"

"What?"

"It's true. Do you know that DBCP, which was banned in 1979, is still found in drinking water?"

"How do you know so many statistics?"

He shrugged. "I just remember them. Am I boring you?"

"No," she said unconvincingly.

He laughed. "Yes, I am. Nobody can be more boring than me when I get on my soapbox. I'm sorry. How would you like to punish me?"

"An afternoon in Bennett should be punishment enough," she said. "Especially Saturday afternoon. Everybody will be there, shopping or going to the movies, or just hanging out by the courthouse. And everybody has known me since I was a little girl and nobody has ever seen you before and they'll all want to know who you are and what you're doing with me. What shall we tell them?"

"You've had death threats and I'm your bodyguard?"

"Very funny. Anyway, you don't look tough enough to be a bodyguard."

"Thank you very much. Are you insulting my physique?"

She blushed. "I didn't mean it that way. I mean you look too nice."

" 'Nice'? As in 'comfortable'? I can see I'm really impressing you."

"I don't think of 'nice' and 'comfortable' as insults. How would you describe me?" she asked, surprised at herself, thinking that was something Marci would say.

"Oh . . . first of all, nice. Very nice. And then . . . comfortable. My kind of girl."

She couldn't tell if he was kidding or not.

"I know!" he said. "We can pretend I'm visiting from some foreign country and I don't speak the language. You'll have to interpret for me."

"But that's ridiculous! I can't do that."

"Why not? I do great imitations."

"Well, I don't. How can I interpret for you?"

"We can figure out a few phrases. That's all you need. You can always say you don't know how to translate something if it gets too hard. Come on, take a chance."

"I don't know."

"Listen, when I was about thirteen I used to pretend I was blind when my mother made me shop with her. I'd hold on to the sleeve of her coat and look around all vacant-eyed. She'd get real annoyed, and when I'd trip over curbs, she'd say, 'Will you *stop* that?' and everybody would look at her like she was a witch, treating a poor blind boy that way."

"I don't believe you."

"It's true. You can ask her."

"Will I get the chance?"

"Sure. If you want to. Do you?"

"If she won't cry over me."

"She might."

They were entering Bennett, and as Robin had predicted, the streets were crowded with shoppers.

"This is our historic main street," she said, driving slowly down it, "with Krogers on the right and the A & P on the left. Further down is the Bijou Theater, where we get such third-run favorites as *Tarzan and the Pygmies* and *Revenge of the Cattle Rustlers*. Over there is the Crest Café, fondly known as the Crust Café, where you can get food poisoning any day of the week. I know this must seem provincial to a world traveler like yourself, but you did come to this country to soak up some of its atmosphere, right?"

"Da," he said.

Robin parked the car at the end of Main Street, since all the closer spaces were already taken. "This scheme of yours will never work," she told him.

"Trust me. I won't let you get out of the car until you know just what to do. Have you got a piece of paper?"

Robin retrieved a school notebook from the back seat and watched as Rick sounded out nonsense phrases and wrote them down. Then he made Robin repeat them, telling her what they were supposed to mean, until she'd memorized them.

"This is insane," she said. "How would I know how to speak this language, anyway?"

"It was your grandfather's native language. You learned

it at his knee as a child and it's come back to you from listening to me. I can be the grandson of one of your grandfather's old buddies."

"My grandfather's name was Herb Clayton. How foreign does that sound to you?" Robin asked.

"So they changed his name at Ellis Island. They did that all the time." He looked at her. "Okay. If you don't want to, we won't. I just thought it would be fun. A little harmless fun. Not hurting anybody. Most people spend their lives . . ."

"All right, all right!" she said, grinning. "Do you always get your own way?"

He opened the car door. "If I don't, it's not for lack of trying."

They walked back toward the center of town.

"What should I call you?" Robin asked.

"How about Litvark? That could cover a lot of countries."

"I'll take your word for it. I never heard of it."

"Me, neither. That's what I mean."

"Look alive. Here comes your first test—it's my friend Marci."

Ahead of them, Marci was coming out of the dime store, a package in her hand. She saw Robin and waved. "Hi, Rob," she called.

They came up to her. "Hi, Marci. This is Litvark. He's a friend of my grandfather's from overseas. He's visiting relatives in Jefferson and came down to see us. He doesn't speak any English. Litvark, *doosel vinyee Marci.*"

Rick took Marci's hand, bent, and kissed it. Marci looked at Robin, startled. "Wow!"

"That's the way they do it in, uh, in his country," Robin said.

"Is *he* the company you were expecting? I can see why you didn't want to share him. He's adorable." She lowered her voice. "I bet I could get along with him without using any words." She laughed. "Am I glad he can't understand me! Say, how come you can talk to him?"

"Funny you should ask. I learned the language from my Grandfather Clayton when I was little. It's amazing how fast it came back when I started talking to Litvark."

Rick stood on the hot sidewalk beaming at the two girls, his hands clasped in front of him.

"Why don't you bring him dancing at the Pavilion tonight?" Marci asked. "He'd sure give Ivan something to think about. Can he dance?"

"I don't know. I'll ask him. *Yertle meesuk tappi-tappi, Litvark?*"

Rick's eyes lit up, and he launched into a long string of gibberish, enthusiastically waving his hands. It was all Robin could do to keep from giggling.

"Gee, I'm sorry, Marci. He has to head back to Jefferson after dinner. But he said he's the national champion of native dancing in his country. If you'd like to see some of the native dances, he'd be glad to show you."

"There's plenty of things I'd like him to show me, but native dancing isn't one of them. For goodness' sakes, Rob, he's gorgeous. I hope you run into Ivan before what's-his-name has to leave."

"I wouldn't mind that at all."

"Well, too bad about the Pavilion. Why don't you come

anyway, if he leaves in time? I gotta go." She held up her package. "My mother forgot the balloons for Billy's party. The little monsters'll pop them all in the first ten minutes anyway, for goodness' sakes. Tell Gorgeous goodbye for me."

Robin interpreted "goodbye" to Rick and he looked at Marci, stricken. He bent over her hand again, murmuring sad sounds as he kissed it goodbye.

"Oh, Rob, this guy is too good to be true. He could sure teach the boys around here a few things. How well do you know him?"

"We've just met."

"Well, if he was staying at my house, I'd make it a point to get to know him better."

Rick said something with a questioning intonation to Robin.

"He wants to know what we're talking about," she told Marci. "I'm going to tell him you said it was nice to meet him. See you later."

Marci gave Rick a twiddling wave with her fingers and a voluptuous smile and went off down the street.

"What's the big idea?" Rick asked. "I would have gone dancing at the Pavilion. Especially with Marci. We wouldn't need words to communicate."

"All you can do are folk dances, remember? Anyway, I don't want to be stuck interpreting all night. It's hard!"

"Who's Ivan?"

"Just somebody I used to go out with."

"Used to? What happened?"

"We had a difference of opinion over something. Pay

attention, here comes Miss Emerson, my first-grade teacher. She's retired now and a little hard-of-hearing, so this should be easier than it was with Marci."

"Robin, dear, how are you?" Miss Emerson said, taking Robin's hands in her old soft ones. "And who is this handsome young man? I thought I knew all the Bennett boys. Had every one of them in my class at one time or another."

"He's not from Bennett, Miss Emerson," Robin said loudly. "He's visiting us from Europe. He doesn't speak any English. But let me introduce you to him." She turned to him. "Litvark, *doosel vinyee Miss Emerson.*" Rick bent and kissed Miss Emerson's hand.

"Ooh," she said, flustered. "How charming. Such lovely Old World manners. What a shame our boys don't have them. What did you say his name was?"

"Litvark," Robin said, raising her voice.

"Litvark," mused Miss Emerson. "What an unusual name. Where did you say he was from?"

Robin mumbled something.

"What's that, dear?"

Robin mumbled louder.

Miss Emerson frowned. "Oh, yes. A lovely place. I hope to get there someday. Well, I must get on with my errands. How nice to see you, Robin dear. Say hello to your father and your grandmother for me, won't you? And tell Litvark I enjoyed meeting him."

Robin interpreted, Rick kissed Miss Emerson's hand again, and she fluttered off across the street.

They continued their stroll, occasionally stopping for Robin to introduce Rick to someone.

"I can't believe we're pulling this off," she said. "Why don't we go over to the Crust and reward ourselves with a lemonade. The acid usually kills any harmful bacteria in it."

"Good idea," Rick said. "My lips are getting chapped."

The inside of the café seemed dim after the brightness outside. When Robin's eyes adjusted, she saw Ivan and Bobby sitting in the front booth, eating hamburgers.

She turned to Rick. "Are you sure you want a lemonade?"

"Positive. Why?"

"Get ready to be Litvark again. There's some people I know in the front booth and they're not going to let me go by without talking to them. Let's get it over with."

They passed Ivan's booth. "Hey, Robin!" he called. "How you doin'?"

"I'm fine."

"Haven't seen you since before school got out."

"That's right," she said.

"Aren't you going to introduce us to your friend there?"

"Of course. This is Litvark. He's visiting from Europe. He doesn't speak any English. Litvark, *doosel vinyee Ivan.*"

Rick's eyebrows went up. He clicked the heels of his boots together and held his hand out to Ivan. Ivan, looking surprised, took it.

"Litvark, doosel vinyee Bobby."

Rick clicked his heels again and shook hands with Bobby.

"So, what are you and this Aardvark character up to?" Ivan asked.

"His name is Litvark. I'm just showing him Bennett.

We got hot and came in for a lemonade. Nice seeing you, Ivan. *Kummi, Litvark."* She started to walk away.

"Wait a minute, wait a minute," Ivan said. "You and Lardass want to come out to the Pavilion tonight?"

"I told you his name is Litvark. We can't. He's going back to Jefferson tonight."

"I could come and pick you up after he goes."

Robin smiled involuntarily. "No, thanks."

"It's on my way. No big deal. I'm willing to be friends, if you think you can handle it without getting all sticky about me again." He glanced at Bobby.

"Sticky! About you? I haven't regretted breaking up with you for one second! I should have done it sooner!" She stormed to the back of the café, pulling Rick behind her, but she heard Ivan say to Bobby, his voice raised so she'd have to hear him, "Poor kid. She's still not over me. The best she can do is some heel-knocking Nazi who doesn't even speak English."

Rick started to turn back.

"You can't understand English, remember?" Robin hissed, pushing him into the last booth.

"So that's Ivan," Rick said. "Miss Emerson was right. No Old World manners there. May I ask what it was you saw in him?"

"He was just somebody to go out with," Robin said, looking at the menu she knew by heart. "It was nothing. I don't know why he's making such a production about it. He can't stand anybody to know I didn't go into mourning when we broke up."

"If you ask me, he still has the hots for you."

"Oh, stop. I wouldn't go out with him again if he came gift-wrapped." And she meant it.

Nikki arrived at their table, her pad in hand. "Hi, Nikki. I want a lemonade."

"Make it two," Rick said.

"You want two lemonades?" Nikki asked Rick, with a resounding gum-crack.

"No. I want one, and she wants one." He pointed at Robin. "That makes two."

Nikki winked at him. Turning to Robin, she said, "Your taste's improving." She wrote something on her pad and went away.

"I don't have to stay for dinner. If you'd rather go to the Pavilion with your friends, I can leave early."

"No!" Robin said loudly. "I mean, no. I don't want to go to the Pavilion. I really don't. I'd rather have dinner with you. It's like what you said on the phone about picking who you want to be friends with more carefully now that you're sick. I feel that way already. It's important who I spend time with if I don't have any time to waste."

"What about Marci?"

"I see plenty of Marci. She's always around."

"Well, all right. I'll stay if you're sure you want me to."

"You want me to beg you?" she asked.

"Okay."

She balled up her napkin and threw it at him.

By the time they left the café, Ivan and Bobby were gone. The sun was slanting down Main Street, but it was still strong and hot. They walked slowly back to the car, thankful not to meet anybody Robin knew. They had both had enough of Litvark. "Next time you can be blind," Robin said. "It would be easier."

"For you, maybe. Next time I want to be looking right in Ivan's face when I punch him in the mouth."

She smiled up at him. "I just love your Old World charm."

Libby met them at the door when they got back to the farmhouse. "Hi. Miss Emerson just called and said she'd seen you in town with some foreigner and how delightful he was. You want to clue me in?"

So they came in and sat at the kitchen table and told her all about Litvark and she laughed so hard she couldn't get her breath and Robin had to pound her on the back. As she went about preparing supper, every now and then she'd burst into a ripple of giggles, say, "Litvark!" and have to take off her glasses to wipe her eyes.

"Rick," Libby said, joining them at the table over glasses of iced coffee, "I'd like to hear more about this organic farming. That's the way I've always done my little kitchen garden—I just thought I was being old-fashioned, but I dare you to find better vegetables. I use manure from Elsie and the chickens and mulch it over with straw to keep the weeds down. I keep ladybugs for the insects, and if I have to, I go out and pull those awful tomato worms off by hand. Could you really do that on a whole big farm?"

"I believe you could," he said. "Not quite how you're doing it in your garden, but there are ways."

Robin excused herself and went upstairs. After she'd

washed her hands and brushed her hair, she stood at her window looking out over the rows of young corn and soybean plants in the fields. She'd always imagined she could actually sense the movement of the earth in the summer when the crops were growing so fast they even looked different from day to day.

"I thought I heard Daddy come in," she said, returning to the kitchen.

"He went to clean up," Libby answered. "You okay?"

"I'm fine," Robin said as Will came into the kitchen. He took two beers from the refrigerator and offered one to Rick. Libby thought only vulgar women drank beer, and Robin didn't like the way it tasted, but she took the first cold swallow from her father's and made a wish on it, the way she'd done since she was little. Tonight her wish was not just for herself but for Rick, too.

Over dinner, Libby told Will about Litvark and warned him that people might ask about their foreign visitor. Will laughed in a way Robin could hardly remember. The last time must have been when her mother was alive.

As Libby and Robin picked up the dessert dishes, Rick rose to help. "I'll wash and you dry," he said to Robin. "Libby and your father probably have something better to do. After all, it's Saturday night."

Libby looked at Will appraisingly. "What do you think?" she asked him. "We haven't been out of here in the evening in I don't know how long. You want to go to a movie?"

"You want to, Libby?" Will asked.

"You know me," she said. "I'd go to a dogfight just to have something to do. Let me change my shoes."

"You kids want to go with us?" Will asked.

"Thank you, sir," Rick said, "but I have to be getting home soon. I've really enjoyed my day here. I hope Robin can come over to Moreland and visit us sometime."

"If she'd like to," Will said, looking at her.

"I would," she answered.

Robin and Rick were still doing the pots and pans which couldn't go in the dishwasher when Libby and Will left for the movies. Rick sprinkled cleanser in the sink as Robin hung up the damp dish towels.

"My mother always says the dishes aren't done till the sink's scrubbed," he said.

"Do you have to leave now?" she asked him as he finished the job.

"Not this minute," he said. "I can stay for a while. Why don't we sit on the porch and watch the sun go down?"

They sat together on the white wicker love seat as the bright flare of sunset threw the furrows of new plants into high relief. With one last burst of color, the rosy sky lingered its way through mauve and lavender to purple and dark blue. They watched it silently, holding hands.

"Hard to find a better show than that," Rick finally said.

Tears pricked Robin's eyes. "Night makes me sad now. I remember a poem we had in English—Dylan Thomas, about raging against the dying of the light. It was about death. I understand it better now."

He put his arms around her. "Yes. But we'll all feel that way sooner or later."

"I want it to be later," she said, pressing her wet face against his shoulder.

"Of course. But didn't you pay more attention to that sunset than you would have if you thought you'd be looking at them for a hundred more years?"

"Don't lecture me. I'm scared. I don't want to die."

"I'm sorry. All right. I won't try to cheer you up. Let's both sit here and be as miserable as we can."

After a few minutes Robin's sniffling stopped. She lay against Rick's chest, motionless. Then she sat up. "It's no use. I can't imagine being dead."

He laughed, and so did she. "Why is it so hard to stay gloomy around you?" she asked.

"Today was fun. I wish I didn't have to go home."

"I wish you didn't, too."

They leaned toward each other, a mutual impulse, and kissed, a little glancing kiss that almost missed. Rick put his hand on her cheek. "Let's try that again."

That time it worked much better. Robin didn't feel submerged, the way she had when she kissed Ivan. She felt as if she were soaring.

"Maybe we should save some for next time," Rick said finally, resting her head on his shoulder and stroking her thick hair.

"Moreland's so far away."

"I drive fast." He stood up, pulling her with him. "Walk me to the car."

They stood by the car for a few minutes, kissing again, until Rick got in. Robin leaned her elbows on the open window frame to kiss him one last time.

"I'll call you," he said, starting the engine.

She watched the red taillights leave the driveway and turn down the road to the highway. With the dark house quiet behind her, the crickets singing in the lilacs, and the cold stars wheeling overhead, she felt as alone as she had ever been in her life.

Fall

The phone next to Robin's bed rang, waking her up. The phone was new, installed at the end of the summer when she stopped coming downstairs.

"Hello?"

"Hi," Rick said. "It's me. Did I wake you up?"

"It's okay." She nestled the receiver into the pillow next to her ear so she could talk without lifting her head. If she kept very still, the nausea eased.

"Happy Halloween," he said.

"Lucky me. I don't have to worry about a costume tonight. I look like a ghoul without even trying."

"You always look beautiful to me."

"How would you know? You haven't seen me in three weeks." She knew she sounded whiny, but she didn't care.

"You told me not to come, remember? You said you were too sick."

"I knew this would happen. I knew you'd lose interest as you got better and I got worse. Especially when you went away to college."

"Robin, I'm only as far away as Jefferson. I'm at an agricultural college, not a pleasure palace. I've called you every night. You're not being reasonable."

Tears leaked from her eyes, dampening the pillow. "I know. I can't help it. I look awful, I feel awful, I can hardly even get out of bed, and you're surrounded by beautiful college girls who would love to get their hands on you and there's nothing I can do about it." She put her hand over her mouth to keep herself from sobbing.

"I don't *want* any other girls. You're my girl. Can I come see you next weekend?"

"I look so terrible. And I keep throwing up."

"I don't care. I'll wear a blindfold if you want me to."

"Okay. If you're sure you can stand it, come whenever you want. You always know where you can find me. What are you going to do tonight?"

"The house is having a party, but I don't know if I'll go. I don't have a costume to wear."

"Go. I want you to go. You can think up a costume. Have fun. You should. Life is short. Remember?"

"I remember. I'll talk to you tomorrow. Good night, G.R."

"Good night."

The effort of hanging up the receiver was too much for Robin, so she lay next to it, listening to it buzz, imagining the long thin wire between her and Rick stretching across all those miles of harvested fields, stubble, and empty furrows, ending at a silent telephone in an empty room.

There was a knock on the door. Libby opened it and stuck her head in. "Hi, sugar pie. You need anything?"

"Could you hang up the phone for me?"

"Sure." She walked over to the bed and hung it up. "I thought I heard your phone ring. Rick?"

Robin nodded.

"You're a lucky girl, you know that? That is one fine boy, and he treats you like a princess."

"I know, I know. You say that all the time. I sure am lucky. Some princess. More like the wicked witch."

"Minerva's downstairs with her grandchildren. She brought them by to trick-or-treat. You want to see them? I could bring them upstairs. They're just darling. The little girl is a black cat, with a tail and ears, and whiskers on her face. And the boys, one's a pirate and the other one's somebody with a cape. It might cheer you up."

"No. I'm too scary-looking for little kids to see. Especially when I . . ." She grabbed the metal basin on the bed and retched into it, heaving and heaving for a spoonful of bile. The vomiting, bad enough alone, hurt even more because of the ulcers inside Robin's mouth, another side effect of the chemotherapy.

Libby soothed Robin's face with a damp washcloth when she lay back on her pillow, clammy and exhausted, then washed out the basin and brought it back.

"Can you sleep now, doll baby?"

Robin nodded, her eyes already closing.

When she woke, Libby was sitting in the armchair, knitting on a sweater for Will. "Hi," Libby said. "Have a good snooze?"

"I don't have a good anything anymore."

"This won't last forever. You'll feel better one of these days."

"Probably because I'll be dead."

"Robin!"

"It's true. I'd just as soon be dead, anyway. I can't even stand to look at myself—a bag of bones with circles under my eyes. And nobody told me that when your hair falls out it isn't just the hair on your head. It's *all* your hair."

"You look nice and smooth."

"Oh, Libby, I look like a plucked chicken! I don't even have eyebrows!"

"You want me to draw some on? I could do that if it would make you feel better."

"No. Never mind. They'd just rub off on the pillow. Anyway, you're the only person who ever sees me and you're used to it." Robin wouldn't let even Marci, who had been a faithful visitor all summer, come anymore.

"I don't mind the way you look," Libby said.

Another paroxysm of vomiting overcame Robin, and when Libby had again cleaned her, she sat on the edge of the bed holding Robin's hand in hers. "I know that book said you could help yourself get better by thinking positive thoughts, but it seems to me there's a time and a place for some negative ones. Even if they are supposed to attract negative things."

"I wasn't thinking any negative thoughts when I got leukemia," she said weakly, her mouth burning. "How did that get attracted to me?"

"I wish I knew. You want me to turn on the TV? Maybe there's something on that would make you laugh."

"Go ahead. At least you can watch it." She turned her head on the pillow. "How come Daddy never comes up and sits with me if I look so nice and smooth?"

Libby sighed. "He wishes he could, but he just can't. It's too hard for him to have to watch you being so sick. But he always comes in and tells you good night."

"That's when the lights are out. He doesn't have to look at me."

"That's so. But he keeps on coming. Don't be angry with him, Robin. He's doing the best he can." She flipped the channels around until she found a comedy, then adjusted the volume and went back to the armchair.

Libby chuckled and knit, and Robin lay frowning in bed. "I never thought I'd die a virgin."

Libby turned to her. "What?"

"You heard me. I don't want to die a virgin. It's not fair. You got three husbands and I'm not going to get any."

"Well, it averages out pretty well," Libby said, smiling. "One and a half for each of us. You can have the first one and I'll take the last one, and we can split the second."

Robin pushed at the pillows under her head. "You told me about the first one, and I knew Herb, but I don't know anything about the second one. What was he like?"

"Let's see." Libby put her knitting in her lap. "He was tall, dark, and handsome. He really was. Seems funny my first two husbands were so outrageously handsome and my third one was short and bald and overweight. But God put no better man on this earth than Herb. It took me too long to learn that looks aren't everything. Well, anyway. His name was Randall, but nobody called

him that. Everybody called him Lucky. He was a sales-
man and he could sell anybody anything. I guess he sold
himself to me, in a way of speaking. Like most of his
customers, though, I didn't get what I paid for. He may
have been pretty on the outside, but he was mean on the
inside. *Oh,* he was mean. Had to have everything just his
way, no matter how unreasonable that was, or he got
hitting mad."

"He hit you?"

She nodded. "Yes. Yes, he did, I'm ashamed to say. I
protected the boys, though. When Eddie was born, right
after we came home from the hospital, he was lying in
his little basket crying and crying and I didn't know what
to do. I'd changed him and fed him and all that and I felt
like crying myself. Lucky stood over the basket and he
raised his hand like he was going to hit that little baby
and I ran over and stood in front of him and I said, 'Don't
you dare ever *ever* hit any child of mine.' And he didn't.
He hit me instead and told me what a terrible mother I
was, but he never laid a hand on either of the boys. It
was a good thing, too, because they both got to be bigger
than him and they would have remembered. Of course,
by the time they were bigger than him, we were divorced. But I stayed with him ten long, stupid years."

"*Why?* Why did you stay with him so long?"

"Oh, honey, things were different in those days. Di-
vorces weren't so common, and maybe we didn't expect
so many things from being married. There were a lot of
people married then who would probably be divorced these
days, but they never even thought about it. You got mar-

ried and you stayed married and you put up with whatever marriage turned out to be for you. Anyway, I'd already been divorced once, and I didn't want to do it twice. Once was shameful enough. Twice and you began to look kind of scandalous. And I had the boys. How was I going to support them if I was divorced? But finally he beat me up so bad he put me in the hospital over nothing—he thought I was flirting with somebody I didn't even know—and then I was afraid he might kill me. So when I got out of the hospital I went to stay with a friend who was keeping the boys for me, and I never went home. I got a job and took care of us. The end." She picked up her knitting.

"What about Herb? When did you meet him?"

"Not too long after that. I met him where I worked. We kept company for a long time before I could think about getting married again, you can imagine. I was pretty gun-shy. But Herb kept asking me, thank goodness, and finally I said okay. So he adopted the boys and together we had Julie and I lived happily ever after with him. I really did."

Robin beat her hand against the blanket.

"What's the matter?" Libby asked.

"All these things that have happened to you. You've had such a full life. I'm not going to."

"Now, you don't know that. Anyway, all those things weren't so great. I wouldn't wish those ten years with Lucky on my worst enemy. Certainly not on you."

"You had so many events. I'm not going to have anything except the preparation part, the being-a-child part.

You can be so calm about dying because you've had a life. I'm going to have to die with only a glimpse of it."

"Who says you're going to die? Nobody's said that. And who says I'm calm about death? I'm not crazy for the idea either. And as far as all those events, there were times when I would have welcomed death. It only sounds interesting now because we know how it turned out. At the time, I didn't know I was going to get away from Lucky, or that I would get Herb. All I knew was I was stuck with this crazy, dangerous man, and I didn't see any way out. I've had a hard life, honey plum. Don't you forget it. I've lost all my children. To wars and disease and accidents; things I was helpless against. I've lost Herb. Just because it's life doesn't mean it's always good."

"No kidding."

Libby put her knitting down and took Robin's hand. "But it isn't all bad, either. Things change. If I could tell you, right now, that you were going to get all better and live to be ninety years old, wouldn't that affect the way you're feeling?"

"Of course. I'd see this as temporary. I can survive anything if I know it's temporary."

"My point is, it might be. Those awful years with Lucky were temporary, even if I didn't know it at the time, and my life was much better after that."

Robin looked at her grandmother. The idea was fragrant with possibilities. She felt so wretched she was sure she was going to die—of the treatment, if not the disease. But maybe this *was* temporary. People did get better. Rick was better. Maybe he was on the way to being cured. Maybe she was, too.

"You ready for a trip to the bathroom?" Libby asked her.

"What?"

"Bathroom. Clean nightgown. Snack. You ready for any of those yet?"

"No to food. But yes to the bathroom. And a fresh nightgown sounds good. It might make me feel better."

"That's my girl," Libby said, helping Robin out of bed.

"Rick's coming next Saturday. Do you think you could draw me some eyebrows then? And find me something to wear on my head? Not a wig, they look so fake. A cap or a bonnet or a scarf, or something." She leaned against Libby, resting from the effort of getting up.

"Well, sure. How about one of those frilly nightcaps? How about a beret? What kind of a mood do you want to set?"

"How about a witch's hat?" Robin asked.

"None of that, now," Libby said. "Positive thoughts, remember?"

They started across the room. "Okay," Robin said. "Let's see. I'm saving money on shampoo. I don't tie up the telephone anymore. You don't have to worry about where I am or who I'm with." She looked at Libby. "That's the best I can do."

When Rick arrived on Saturday, Robin was sitting up in bed wearing a ruffled flannel nightgown that camouflaged her thinness. Libby had helped her put on makeup so that she had eyebrows and some color in her face, and she wore an old-fashioned nightcap with a ribbon running through it.

Rick kissed her cheek. "You look great! What's all this ghoul business?" He sat on the edge of her bed and held her hand.

"You look great, too. You look wonderful. So collegiate." He wore a sweatshirt in his school colors, with a crest on the front. "How's school?"

"School's terrific. And being away from home is better than terrific. I'll never get tired of that. But, God, I've missed you. How are you?"

"Better, I think. I don't feel sick so much of the time, at least. What's it like outside? I hate not being able to go out."

"It feels like November. It's chilly and we've had hard frost the last few nights. And the sun is strong and bright—the kind that looks warm when you see it out the window, but is cold when you go outside."

"I was too sick to watch much of the harvest. I always hate the way the fields look afterwards; so dead and stripped and bare. They're prettier in the winter when they're under snow."

"That's funny. I've always liked the way they look in fall—like they're taking a well-earned rest."

She shook her head. "I like spring, with all the new little plants just starting up. And summer, when everything's green and big, and the fields look so full. I hate fall. When I first got sick, I had the feeling I would die in the fall when everything else is dead, too."

"I don't think you're going to make it, G.R."

"I hope not. At least not this fall."

"When I first got sick, I thought I would die in the

spring. Everything else was starting out fresh. It seemed a good time for me to go on to something new, too."

"What did you think you'd be starting?"

He frowned. "I don't know. I like the idea of reincarnation. I hate to think of being gone forever. But maybe where you go is so good you don't want to come back. I wish I knew."

"You think you go somewhere? Maybe it's just all black, lights out, the end."

"I want to think you go somewhere, so that's what I think. Why not believe what makes you feel best?"

"I hate ambiguity." She lay back on her pillows. "Tell me a story."

"A story? What about?"

"A place where this boy and this girl are crazy about each other and they're both healthy at the same time and they live happily ever after."

"You just told the story. I'm no good at stories. How about the quote of the week?"

"Okay. What is it this week?"

" 'I'm not afraid to die. I just don't want to be there when it happens.' Woody Allen."

She laughed. "I wish I'd said that."

Libby came in the door with a tray bearing a pot of tea and a big pear cobbler. She put it down on top of the dresser. "Will's through for the day, and he's coming up to have tea with us."

Robin's eyes widened, but Libby gazed levelly back at her.

After Will had shaken hands with Rick, and kissed

Robin, he sat down in the armchair facing the foot of the bed, positioned so he couldn't look directly at Robin. Libby poured tea, sliced the cobbler, and passed the plates around.

"You enjoying school?" Will asked Rick, taking a strand of baler twine from his pocket and beginning a string of knots.

"Yes, sir, I am. Very much."

"Seems odd, going to school to learn how to farm. I learned everything I know watching my father and my grandfather. Once in a while, I get a tip from a neighbor or from the county agent. The rest of it I learned by doing."

"Ag school's got its place, but I'm sure real farming can teach you more than all the textbooks in the world. Sometimes I want to dump everything, jump on a tractor, and just start *doing* it."

Will smiled, pocketed the twine, and took a bite of his cobbler.

"I brought you some issues of that magazine I get, *The New Farm.*" Rick took several magazines from his backpack and handed them to Will. "I thought you might like to look at them."

Will leafed through one of them. "Huh! Here's an article on a farmer using draft horses to pull his implements. Draft horses!"

"It may sound old-fashioned," Rick said, "but horses are low-cost, self-reproducing, and you can grow their fuel. And they give you back organic fertilizer. You can't say that about a forage harvester."

"Even my grandfather didn't use draft horses," Will said.

"I'm not saying it would work for everybody, but it's something to think about."

"You're quite a believer in alternative agriculture, aren't you?" Will asked.

"Yes, sir," Rick said. "I know it sounds drastic, but I think it's the only answer to saving our soil." He hesitated, looking embarrassed. "My father says I'm worse than a missionary."

"Don't worry about it. I'd be interested to read these magazines." He flipped through them while he ate his dessert.

Robin sipped her tea carefully, watching as Rick had seconds of cobbler and talked to Libby about college. She was content just to look at him after not seeing him for so long.

Since midsummer, when the combined effects of her illness and its treatment had caused her to quit her job and remain at home, her days had passed between stupor and misery, with only occasional up periods. Marci, sometimes accompanied by Bobby, became her most frequent and most appreciated visitor besides Rick. She brought gossip and funny stories and flowers from her garden, as well as the comfort of not being afraid to be honest. Her settled contentment and her ability to make drama from small daily incidents, the traits that had once irritated Robin, made Marci wonderful company.

Rick had been right about the responses of her friends— some were too solicitous, calling and visiting until she began to suspect some morbid interest prompted them. Others ignored her, but she had no trouble relating to their fear. Ivan had been to see her once, bringing a sentimental card that read, in lavender script, "A Get-Well Wish to My Niece." She'd almost laughed at how typical it was of him not to read past the "Get Well," but she'd been too touched by his awkward sympathy.

When Robin's preoccupations were reduced to trying to find a position that didn't hurt her sharp, sensitive bones, and trying to avoid tipping her precarious balance from lethargy to nausea, she had no wish to inflict them on Marci—it was bad enough to do it to Libby and Rick— and she'd asked Marci to stop coming. Soon afterwards she'd made the same request of Rick. It was too hard on her to be so sick in front of him.

How marvelous it was to have company again.

"Now, Robin, I see you lying back there," Libby said. "Are you getting tired?"

"A little. But it's all right. I like having everybody up here."

"We'll stay another few minutes, but you're making such good progress the past few days, we don't want to cause you a setback." Libby began gathering up the cups and plates. "Come on, Will. Let's give Robin a little more time with Rick. She's getting tired."

Will stood up, holding the magazines in one hand, his finger stuck in a page. He held out the other hand to Rick. "It's good to see you again. Come back soon." He kissed Robin and walked out the door.

Libby picked up the tray. "Come down and visit with me some more before you head back to Jefferson, Rick."

"I will." Rick closed the door after her.

Sitting back on the bed again, he removed his shoes,

then swung his legs up on top of the bedspread. He lay down next to Robin and pulled her against him. Under his hands, he could feel her bones, like twigs.

"I wish I could get in there with you," he said.

"I wish you could, too. One thing I refuse to do is die a virgin."

He laughed. "Maybe I could help you out with that problem."

"Are you volunteering?"

"Any time, lady. Or were you going to hold auditions?"

"I hadn't thought of that, but it's a good idea."

"I thought I was first choice," he said.

"If I'm not going to consider anybody else, I'll need some references."

"I could get a couple."

"From who?" she asked.

"Nobody you know."

"Some of those college girls, I bet."

"Come on, G.R. I'm only teasing. You're the only girl for me. There's nobody else."

"But there was, wasn't there?"

"Well, a long time ago. Before I got sick."

"Who was she?"

"I went pretty seriously with a girl in high school. That's been over a long time. I don't even know what she's doing now."

"Do you miss her? Do you wish you still went with her? I bet she was big and healthy and sexy, wasn't she?"

"Come on, Robin."

"You wouldn't make love to me now, would you? Not on a bet."

"I'd make love with you in a second if I thought you'd enjoy it." He held her close to him. "And you wouldn't have to worry. You know I'd protect you. Us."

"I'm acting stupid," she said, her face pressed against his sweatshirt. "I hate feeling so weak and ugly."

"I know. I hate your being so sick. But you're going to get better and then, look out!"

She smiled into his sweatshirt. "Is that a promise?"

"It's a promise."

They lay quietly together for a while, their arms around each other. Then she felt him shifting his weight, getting ready to release her.

"Don't go! I don't want you to go already! It seems like you just got here."

"It'll be dark soon and I have a long drive. And you need to rest."

Robin held him tighter. "It seems like I started getting worse almost from the first time you came to see me. Remember that day? That silly business with Litvark? Wasn't that fun? And then the next week I started the beetle squeezings and it's been downhill since."

"So now it's time for you to go uphill. We have a lot of fun to make up for."

"I don't know why you keep coming around. Why don't you get a normal girlfriend and forget about me?"

"Because I don't want to. I love you. I've been as sick as you are now, more than once. I know how it feels. It's the beetle squeezings, Rob. They make you depressed."

"I know, I know. Okay, go. I *am* tired. I'm glad you came, though. When can you come back?"

"Next Saturday okay?"

"Wonderful."

He rolled over on his stomach and kissed her as if she were big and healthy and sexy. "Think that over," he said and sat on the edge of the bed to put his shoes on, while she rested her hand on his back until he stood up.

She was asleep when his car pulled out of the driveway.

The next Saturday when he came to see her she was sitting in the armchair beside her bed, and the Saturday after that she was downstairs in the parlor in a sweatsuit. She was still weak and tired, but her hair was beginning to grow back, a little fuzz.

The following Saturday, even though it was cold and gray outside, she was able to take a short walk with him through the barnyard, and she stopped in the barn to lay her face against Elsie's warm neck.

"I can't come next weekend," Rick told her. "It's Thanksgiving and we're having a houseful of company. I have to be there."

"I'll miss you. Being able to see you is helping me get better. I hope you remember your promise."

"Promise?"

"Oh, I *knew* I couldn't trust you." She hit him in the stomach, but he hardly felt it through his down jacket. He grabbed her fist. "I remember," he said. "You haven't changed your mind?"

"Not a chance."

The weekend after Thanksgiving, it snowed and the roads were too bad for Rick to come. The weekend after that was his fraternity initiation and he couldn't break away, and the one after that he needed to stay at school to study for exams. Talking to him every night on the phone was not enough substitute for seeing him, but he said he'd be able to come sometime between Christmas and New Year's.

Robin was up and dressed most of the day now. She had put on a little weight and had a short cap of hair as well as some sparse eyebrows. Because the weather was so cold and icy, Libby was afraid to let her go outdoors, so she tried to divert Robin with making bread and soup and popcorn, reading aloud over high tea by the fire, playing dominoes, Monopoly, and records.

It made Robin remember the ways she and her mother had passed snowbound days, with jacks and marbles, pillow fights and hide-and-seek, and pirate caves made of blankets over the kitchen table.

Marci had resumed her visits and they helped to relieve Robin's restlessness. It seemed fascinating to hear that there was a new math teacher, even though math was Robin's least favorite subject, that the Bennett Bulldogs were winning all their football games, that Bobby was tantalizing Marci with the promise of something special for Christmas. The life outside her bedroom interested her again.

But still she didn't know the final answer: Was she going to be cured or not? How could she make any decisions, or plans or progress without knowing how long she would be around? She even hesitated to start reading a long book. She knew it was possible for anyone to die suddenly, hit by a bus or by a heart attack, but it wasn't the same. They would die with the illusion of a long life in their minds. She didn't have that luxury.

Winter

The Thursday between Christmas and New Year's Rick arrived on the empty screened porch in a sheepskin coat, his head bare, his cheeks pink from cold. Robin ran down the hall, flung open the door, and threw herself into his arms.

"You're running!" he said, hugging her. "And you have hair!"

"Oh, I'm so glad to see you! Can you stay all day? You have to stay all day. I'm going to bar the doors and not let you out."

He stopped in the parlor long enough to put three gifts under the Christmas tree and hang up his coat. Then he went to the kitchen, where Libby sat reading a magazine, waiting for something to come out of the oven. When she saw him she stood up, dropping the magazine on the floor, and hugged him.

"Merry Christmas, Rick. It's been too long. Was Santa good to you?"

"Very. How about you?"

"You kidding? A mean old lady like me? My stocking's full of sticks and ashes every year." She laughed. "But look what Robin gave me." She pointed to a tall white cage next to the stove. In it, a brilliantly colored parrot sat on a perch gazing lovingly at its reflection in a mirror. "Isn't she a beauty? And she talks, too! You should hear her! Already she says 'Hello, Libby' and 'Wash your hands' and 'Drop the gun.' I'd like to know where she lived before she came here."

Rick went over to the cage. "This is a pretty exotic present. Where *did* you find her, Robin?"

"Mr. Schaeffer at the pet shop found her for me," Robin said. "She likes tropical weather, so we have to keep her next to the stove. I'm trying to teach her to be a good conversationalist, but she likes to give orders more than anything else. I can't tell you what a shock I got when I came in here last night for a snack and heard a voice saying 'Drop the gun!'"

"Has she got a name?" Rick asked.

"Polly, of course," Libby said. "You want a cup of coffee?"

"Sure." He sat down at the kitchen table and Libby put on a pot of coffee as the three of them talked about their holidays. Robin sat holding Rick's hand on her knees, thinking nobody had ever looked as good to her.

"Do you want to take a walk?" Robin asked Rick when he had finished his coffee. "I go out every chance I get. I was so sick of being cooped up."

"I don't like it," Libby said. "Those drugs lower her resistance and I'm afraid she'll catch a cold, but she won't listen to me."

"I'll make her bundle up good. And we won't stay out long," Rick said. "You want to come with us? It's really nice out, crisp and dry. Even too dry to make a good snowball."

"No, thanks. I'd rather stay warm. Lunch in about an hour, so don't go far."

By the time Robin had put on her long underwear, an extra sweater, her down jacket, muffler, mittens, and heavy knitted hat, it was too late to walk very far. She burst out the front door into the frosty air, taking big luxurious gulps of it and dancing on the snowy driveway. The air was so cold, bright crystals of it seemed to snap in front of her eyes.

She stuck her arm through Rick's and hugged it to her side. "I feel like Charlie Brown in that cartoon where his mother gets him all bundled up and he falls over on the sidewalk and is so padded he can't get up. Don't let me fall over."

"I won't. Unless I can go with you."

"O-ho," she said. "Not out here, but any other time and place of your choice."

"Well, I've been thinking about that."

"Have you, now. And what do you think?"

"I'm scheduled for a couple of days in the hospital for tests, at the end of January. Aren't you due for some about the same time?"

"I think so. Why?"

"Well, we could be in Jefferson, if we arrange things right, the two of us, for a few days. *Alone.*"

She stopped walking and put her mittened hands on his cheeks. Pulling his face down to hers, she kissed his cold lips. "I think that's the best idea I've ever heard."

They were starving when they got back to the house. They shed their heavy outerwear in the hall and went to stand before the parlor fire, rubbing their hands together and shivering.

Will joined them there when he came in from his

workshop and they went together into the kitchen for lunch. By now Rick was used to Libby's moment of silent worship and he took Robin's hand, and Will's, in his.

"I have a riddle for you, Mr. Gregory," Rick said as they began their meal. "What's the difference between a pigeon and a farmer?"

"You got me."

"A pigeon can still make a small deposit on a tractor."

Will laughed. "That probably wouldn't mean much to your father, but it's surely something I can identify with."

"Have you read any of those alternative-farming magazines I gave you?" Rick asked.

"Yes. I have. I know you're a true believer, but some of that stuff sounds pretty farfetched to me."

"Not when you consider that the cost of the fossil fuels used to produce chemical fertilizers and pesticides has risen over four hundred percent in the last few years."

"I admire a man who's committed to something, even if I don't agree with him," Will said, smiling. "Anyway, there might be some truth to what you think."

"There's more than *some* truth, Mr. Gregory. There's a lot of truth. It's . . ." Rick noticed Robin and Libby giving each other an amused look. "What?" he asked. "Oh—there I go again. I guess I'm just a zealot. I can't help it."

Robin stood up. "Why don't we take our dessert into the parlor and have it by the fire and the Christmas tree?"

"That's a good idea, Robin," Libby said, getting up, too. "I'll bring the coffee."

"I've eaten so much of Libby's Christmas baking this year, I'm going to have to go on a diet," Will said, taking the last bite of applesauce cake. "What's that under the tree? I thought we'd opened everything already. Maybe Santa came back with a bigger belt for me."

"Those are some things I brought," Rick said. He went to the tree and picked up the gifts, handing one to each of them. "Merry Christmas."

"What a nice surprise," Libby said. "Here I thought we were all through with the fun part, and we get a little bonus. Go on, Will, you first."

Will opened his small, flat, gold-wrapped box to find an envelope. He pulled out a printed certificate. "A year's subscription to *The New Farm*. Thank you, Rick. Maybe I'm not too old a dog to learn a new trick or two."

Rick's gift to Libby was a folding caddy for her knitting. It had compartments for yarn, knitting needles, instruction books, crochet hooks, and other equipment. "This is beautiful," she said. "Lots better than the old plastic bag I carry everything around in now." She got up from her chair and kissed him on the cheek. "Now you wait just a minute. There's something in the kitchen for you." She returned with two Mason jars, which she handed to Rick. "I want you to take these home with you. This is corn relish, and these are spiced crab apples. I put them up myself."

"Thanks, Libby. I wish I could take one of your applesauce cakes home, too. I never ate such good applesauce cake."

"Lucky you. I've got one in the freezer and it's yours. Don't let me forget, when you get ready to leave."

"I won't." He turned to Robin. "Go on. Open yours now."

It was a small box, wrapped in silver paper and topped

with a sprig of holly and a cluster of little red Christmas balls. "It's too pretty to open," she said.

"Okay. You can use it for a paperweight or a door-stop."

She laughed and unwrapped it. Removing the lid, she found, lying on a slice of cotton, a narrow silver bracelet in the shape of a plastic hospital wristband. On the front was engraved GREGORY, ROBIN. "Oh," she said. "It's perfect."

"Let me see," Libby said. "What is it?"

Robin showed her. "That's how Rick learned my name, when we first met. From looking at my hospital band. Where did you ever get such a thing?" she asked him.

"A friend of mine makes jewelry. I had him do it from my design."

She put it on her wrist. "Now I have something for you. Libby helped me a little bit, but I did most of it." From the back of the Christmas tree she pulled a large box tied with green ribbons, and handed it to Rick.

Inside he found a green wool sweater Robin had knit during her long weeks indoors. He held it up to himself. "It looks like a perfect fit," he said.

"That's a good color on you," Libby commented.

"My English teacher says green is the color of hope," Robin said. "I even used green ribbons on the box."

Rick pulled off the sweater he was wearing and put on the new one. He stood up and looked at himself in the mirror over the fireplace. "I look great, if I do say so myself."

"I agree," Robin said.

"Well, now that Christmas is over again," said Libby, "I think I better clean up those lunch dishes."

"And I have to start getting the account books in order for the end of the year," Will said. "I'm sure you two won't miss us."

After Will and Libby had left the room, Robin and Rick sat on the couch, his arm around her shoulders. He looked down at his new sweater. "I didn't know you could knit."

"Neither did I," she said proudly.

They spent the rest of the afternoon playing Trivial Pursuit, which Robin had gotten for Christmas, on the floor in front of the fire. Between games, Robin went into the kitchen to fix hot chocolate. As she stood, waiting for the milk to heat, she looked out the window and thought how much she loved this place, and how much she wanted to see many more winters here. The lure of the wider world had receded. How could she have thought Bennett was too tame and safe to hold her? Now it hardly seemed safe enough.

After dinner, Robin put on her coat, hat, and mittens and walked Rick to his car. He put his gifts on the back seat and opened the passenger door for her. "Get in so I can tell you goodbye properly."

He started the car and turned on the heater, and as they had been aching to do all day, they fell into each other's arms.

When, finally, Robin got ready to go in, Rick said, "As soon as I know the dates for my tests, I'll let you know. Then you can schedule yours for the same time."

"I can hardly wait."

"I'll call you," he said, and drove out to the road. There

was no sadder sight to Robin than red taillights in the dark, leaving her behind.

The plan worked; they were both able to schedule their tests for the last week in January. Libby had even agreed to let Robin drive herself to Jefferson and back. Since she was feeling well and would be in the hospital for tests, not treatment, there was no need for someone else to drive her.

Robin went back to school, a semester behind, but willing to work hard to catch up. The winter was severe, with freezing temperatures and much snow, and as the last week of January approached, Robin became more and more apprehensive about the weather. What if there was a storm on the day she was supposed to go to Jefferson? Libby would never let her drive in a snowstorm. Ordinarily she wouldn't *want* to drive in a snowstorm. But she knew she would drive through any kind of storm, to be with Rick.

It was clear and cracking cold the morning Robin was to leave for the hospital, and when she came downstairs for breakfast, Libby was already fretting to Polly. "I'm going to tell her to postpone those tests, Polly. It's just too cold for her to be driving. Anything could go wrong with her car, and then where would she be? Stuck on the highway getting frozen, that's where."

"Getting frozen. Wash your hands," Polly said.

"Oh, Robin, there you are," Libby said. "Sugar pie, it's so cold, why don't you—"

"I heard what you said to Polly," Robin said, "and nothing's going to happen. Even if I do have car trouble,

I can call Triple A. Or there'd be a highway patrol car along soon, or somebody else would stop and help me."

"Probably some homocidal maniac . . ."

"Don't be such a pessimist. Anyway, I want to get these tests over with. I don't like having them hanging over my head. Besides, I've already gotten all my homework assignments for the days of school I'm going to miss and I've made up two tests in advance, and I'm all packed. It's too much trouble to cancel." Nothing was going to stop her.

"Well, I don't like it," Libby said, putting Robin's breakfast on the table.

"I don't like it," Polly said.

"I know you don't," Robin said. "Both of you. But it'll be okay, I promise."

They heard Will come onto the back porch, stamping the snow from his boots. A gust of frigid air came in the door with him.

"Drop the gun!" Polly yelled.

"Oh, close that door," Libby said. "I don't want Polly to get a draft. Now, Will, you try and talk some sense into Robin. I want her to cancel those tests and wait for a warmer day to go to Jefferson."

"The way the weather's been going," Will said, "she might not get another chance. All these storms we've been having keep coming up out of nowhere. I'd say go now and get it done with."

Libby turned to the stove. "Oh, all right. I know when I'm outnumbered. But I still don't like it."

When she finished her breakfast, Robin kissed her father and grandmother, and had to restrain herself from sprinting to her car. Libby followed her to the garage, her sweater pulled around her, issuing admonitions all the way.

"Drive carefully, the road could be slippery. Don't go too fast. They'll wait for you. Call me when you get there. If it's snowing when you get ready to start back, stay in a hotel. I don't want you to drive in the snow. Robin, are you listening to me?"

"Sure, I'm listening. Goodbye, Libby." She backed out of the garage. Rick was waiting for her and they would have two whole days together.

They planned to go to a motel right after their tests were finished on the second day. Robin had told Libby that she would probably have to spend two nights in the hospital, but in reality there would be only one.

As soon as she checked into the hospital, she called Libby and then began her round of tests. She knew by asking at the information desk that Rick had already arrived, though she didn't see him.

Robin was the only patient in a four-bed room, on the same floor as Rick's private room. Because of the large donations Mr. Winn made to the hospital, Rick always got the same big corner room whenever he was in the hospital.

Robin's favorite nurse, Virginia, told her that the bad weather discouraged many people from coming to the hospital unless it was an emergency. They were frightened of power failures and of being left alone by families who couldn't make it through the storms to visit them and by doctors who couldn't get to them for the same reason.

By midafternoon, Robin was through for the day. She went directly to Rick's room, where she found him playing solitaire on the tightly made bed, wearing the green sweater she had made for him. When he saw her, he jumped up and hugged her. "Where have you been?" he asked. "I've been down to your room ten times and you're never there."

"I came for some tests, remember? So I've been having them."

"Enough with the tests. Come on, let's take a walk and go out for dinner."

"Can we do that? Aren't we supposed to stay in the hospital?"

"Who says? We're not prisoners."

They went out to the nurses' station, Rick leading Robin by the hand. Virginia looked up from a chart she was writing in. "Well, what is this? It appears you two know each other."

"No. I'm just a fast worker," Rick said.

"You better watch out for him, Robin," Virginia said. "This is the boy who refused to take his marijuana for nausea in pill form."

"Purely medicinal," Rick said. "Anyway, when I was taking my 'medicine,' you used to come into my room all the time just to inhale deeply. Robin and I would like to have dinner out if that's okay."

"We'll have to get your doctors to okay it, but I don't think that'll be any problem."

Robin and Rick waited in the lounge while Virginia made the necessary phone calls. As soon as she came to tell them it was all right, they gathered their cold-weather gear, bundled up in the lobby, and left the hospital as giddy as children playing hooky.

The frozen streets looked bleak in the flat light of the oncoming winter sunset, but nothing could dampen their spirits.

"Nothing ordinary for dinner tonight," Rick said. "No pizza, no burgers, no spaghetti. Something special. Something . . . anticipatory."

"What's anticipatory food?" Robin asked.

"Good question. Antipasto?"

They decided on Chinese food, because of the fortune cookies, and found a dimly lit, almost empty red-and-gold restaurant where they fed each other with chopsticks and Rick worked on developing a Chinese accent.

"What do you think?" he asked. "Maybe next time, instead of being Litvark, I can be Chinese."

"Great idea. You certainly *look* Chinese." Cracking open her fortune cookie, Robin read, " 'Look beneath the surface for another world.' What the heck does that mean?"

"How's this for an odd one," Rick said, handing her his fortune. It read 'Produced by the New China Baking Co.' "What do you suppose *that* means?"

Giggling, they went back into the cold dark streets, Robin clinging to Rick's arm, and made their way to the hospital.

They shed their coats and sat in the lounge, pressed together, watching TV.

At ten-thirty, Virginia appeared in the doorway of the lounge. "Probably wouldn't hurt if you turned in," she said. "We won't be coming in during the night to check anything, since you're only in for tests, so you should get a good night's sleep. Your doctors have left orders for sleeping medication, though, if you want it. Sometimes it's hard to sleep in a hospital.''

They both turned down the medication, then shut off the TV and walked together to Robin's empty room. Rick kissed her and said, "Good night. See you tomorrow."

Robin sat on her bed, trying to tie the strings in the back of her cotton hospital gown while her lacy new nightgown, bought in Bennett one day after school and wrapped in tissue paper, waited in her suitcase for tomorrow.

After she'd brushed her teeth, read a magazine, and counted holes in the acoustical tile ceiling, she still wasn't sleepy. Virginia was right: it was hard to sleep in a hospital.

She got up, put on her slippers and, for a robe, another hospital gown with the opening at the front, and left her room, quietly passing the vacant nursing station. Slowly, she pushed open the door to Rick's room.

He lay awake in the dark with his hands behind his head. "Hi," he whispered, coming up on an elbow. "I thought you'd gone to bed."

"I couldn't sleep."

"Me, neither."

She sat down on the side of his bed. "What were you thinking about?"

"You. And the tests. I'm always scared when I come in for them. No matter how good I'm feeling, I'm always afraid they'll find something."

"I know. All those numbers dance around in your head: hemoglobin, platelets, granulocytes. Some too high and some too low."

"You must be cold," he said. "Get in." He pulled the covers back for her and settled her head against his shoulder. "This is when I start praying to all the unknown saints."

"Unknown saints?"

"You have any idea how many saints there are? And how few of them have any kind of reputation? Everybody knows about St. Christopher and St. Francis and St. Jude. But did you ever hear of St. Hyacinth or St. Joseph of Cupertino or St. Philomena? I figure they're the ones most likely to listen since they have less to do."

"I would never have thought of that," Robin said. "I would never have thought of a lot of things unless you made me think about them. How did you ever do it for two years all by yourself?"

"I don't know. You do what you have to do, I guess. But it's been lots easier with you." He rolled over and kissed her.

The planning, the anticipation, the motel reservation, the new nightgown, the Christmas perfume, all proved unnecessary when confronted with love and need and opportunity.

Robin went back to her own room toward morning, leaving Rick asleep. They didn't see each other again until close to four o'clock, when they were both finished with their tests, had seen their doctors, and were ready to leave the hospital.

Rick came to Robin's room holding his suitcase and leaned on the doorframe. "Hi."

She turned from where she was closing her overnight bag on the bed. "Hi, too."

"You look beautiful."

"So do you."

"You ready to go?"

By the time they arrived at the motel, it had begun snowing lightly. After Rick had registered for them and showed Robin where to park, he unlocked the door to their room and opened it for her.

"Oh!" Robin said. "This is luxurious. It must have cost a lot."

"What's money for? There's nothing I'd rather spend it on." He closed the door and their arms went around each other, clinging so hard it almost hurt.

After a time Robin disentangled herself. "I've got to call Libby. She thinks I'm spending tonight in the hospital and I don't want her to call me there and find out I've gone."

"What do you think she'd say if she knew where you were?" Rick pulled off Robin's wool cap and tossed it on the bed.

"I don't know. She loves you and she understands about people who love each other. And she knows I worry about not having enough time. I hope she'd be sympathetic."

Robin sat down on the bed and dialed home. "Hi, Libby, it's me . . . Fine, how are you and Daddy? . . . Everything looks okay so far, but not all the tests are back . . . Oh, it's starting to snow a little . . . You'll probably get it before long . . . I promise, I won't try to drive home if it's snowing. I'll put up in a motel until it stops." She winked at Rick. "Okay . . . see you tomorrow, I hope. Bye."

"You want to go eat first, or what?" he asked after she had hung up.

"Or what."

When they were ready to go to dinner, it was snowing much harder, so they went only as far as the steak house across the road. There was a fire in the dining-room fireplace, and candles on the table, and Robin declared it an altogether satisfactory place to have a celebration dinner. After dinner, they ran back through the snow to their own warm, private place.

They lay snuggled together in the bed, blankets pulled closely around them and, in the pale drowsy light from the bedside lamp, listened to the wind blow outside.

"Libby always says I named my chickens wrong. She says the rooster should be named Happy, since there's only one of him and six of them."

She felt Rick's smile against her cheek. "One of you and one of me is enough to make me happy."

Robin sighed contentedly. "I haven't heard a quote of the week in a long time," she said. "Have you run out of them?"

"No. I have a perfect one. 'In the depths of winter, I finally learned that within me there lay an invincible summer.' Camus said that. I hope it turns out to be true of me."

"What do you mean?"

"The tests," he said in a flat voice. "They've never been this bad. I'm going to have to start chemo again."

She lifted his face in her suddenly cold hands. "Why didn't you tell me sooner?" she whispered.

"I couldn't." His voice cracked. "Oh, God, why now?"

He wept into her palms and she felt her brief, bright joy slip through her fingers with his tears.

Robin hardly remembered the drive home. When she came into the kitchen from the garage, Libby took one look at her face and said, "What is it? You told me the tests looked all right. What didn't you tell me?"

Robin began to cry for the first time since Rick had told her, and the force of her sobs frightened her as well as Libby. Libby guided her to the sofa in the parlor and sat holding her until she had calmed enough to speak.

"It's Rick. He's had a relapse. He has to start chemotherapy again." Her voice was muffled against the cushion of Libby's bosom. "What will I do if something happens to him?" Fresh tears started. *"Why?* Why can't he just get well, and I get well, and we can live and be happy together? Why does it keep being so hard and so awful?" The words came out jerkily, with great sobs between them. "Why does it have to keep getting worse?"

She sat up, her face red and contorted, her eyes streaming. "I don't believe there's a reason for everything," she shouted. "I don't believe God tempers the wind to the shorn lamb. I don't believe God's paying any attention at all!" She jumped up and ran up the stairs, weeping so hard she staggered against the banister.

Libby sat motionless on the couch, tears slipping down her own cheeks.

When Will came in for lunch, Libby told him about Rick. He closed his eyes for a moment; then they sat down at the table, where they ate silently, without Robin.

"I have to go to town," Will said when he had finished pushing his food around on his plate. "Anything I can get for you?"

"Nothing you can find in a store," she said. "Can't you postpone it? I don't like the look of the weather."

"Like I told Robin, better go while I can." He pulled on his coat. "I'll stay in town if it gets bad, and wait it out."

After he had left, the clouds closed in lower and darker and the wind rose to whistle around the corners of the house. Libby turned on all the downstairs lights; this was one day she wasn't going to worry about the electric bill. She kept looking at the clock, timing when Will would get to town so she could quit worrying about him.

Robin came downstairs just as it started to snow again. There were no beginning flurries; the flakes simply poured so heavily from the sky that the outbuildings were almost instantly obscured.

"You want some cocoa?" Libby asked.

"Sure," Robin said, and sat down, folding her hands on the table in front of her. Libby put two cups of cocoa on the table and sat down, too.

The silence settled around them as the cocoa grew cold in the cups. Outside, the snow hurled itself against the house. When the telephone rang, they both jumped before Libby went to answer it.

"That was your father," she said, returning from the parlor. "He's going to stay at Raymond's in town tonight. The weather's too bad to try to get home." She wandered around the kitchen, emptying the dishwasher, refolding the towels, wiping the already clean counter. Finally, she scrubbed two potatoes and put them in the oven.

"We might as well have an early supper," she said. "Then we can get in bed with the electric blankets turned up high and listen to the TV. That sound all right to you?"

Robin looked at Libby as if she were trying to read her lips. Then she got up, put on her coat, mittens, and scarf, and went out the back door.

She fought her way across the barnyard against the wind and the wild, icy snowflakes. After wrestling the barn door open, she wedged herself inside and slammed it behind her. Panting, she leaned against the door, resting in the quiet warmth of the barn. The chickens strutted around, clucking softly to themselves, and Elsie shifted gently in her stall.

She hung her scarf and mittens on a nail, before filling pans with water and chicken mash and replenishing Elsie's food and water. Then she took off her coat and milked Elsie. When she'd poured the milk into a stainless-steel can and sealed it, she leaned against a post, watching her animals eat. Libby would be wondering what had happened to her, but she couldn't make herself go outside and struggle against the blizzard; she was sick of struggle.

She kicked the milking pail into the barn wall and screamed, "It's not fair!"

The chickens raised their heads and looked at her with their angry little eyes. Elsie looked over her shoulder at the commotion.

Robin kicked the pail again, and this time the chickens scattered for cover behind the machine parts and sacks of feed.

"It's not fair, it's not fair, it's not fair!" she screamed. "I don't want to die! I don't want Rick to die! I hate this!" She ran between the obstacles the length of the barn, kicking the pail and watching it ricochet. The chickens squawked from their corners and Elsie stamped her feet. "Make it stop, make it stop! I can't stand any more!"

She stumbled as she kicked at the bucket, and caught herself against Elsie's flank. With her cheek pressed against the cow's smooth, warm side, Robin burst into a torrent of tears. Elsie stood still, as if she understood.

When her sobbing slowed, Robin hung on to Elsie, resting in the hay-scented hush. Gradually she raised her head and, wiping her eyes on her sleeve, retrieved her coat, scarf, and mittens. She stood for a moment by the door, relishing the timeless feeling in the barn; then pushed it open and went back into the storm.

She came into the kitchen, a whirlwind of snowflakes eddying around her.

"Everything all right out there?" Libby asked, helping her off with her wet things.

"Fine," Robin said.

After the supper dishes had been washed and put away, Libby said, "I don't know about you, but I'm tired of looking at snow. You want to come watch TV in my bed?"

"Maybe, in a while," Robin said from where she sat tracing a pattern on the kitchen table.

"Come on, honey. Just about anything's better if there's somebody keeping you company."

"Okay." She stood up and her closed face pierced Libby's heart.

In flannel nightgowns and wool socks, they arranged themselves in Libby's big bed with the carved bedstead, piling up pillows, making room for books and knitting. The TV played something neither of them was interested in, and its sound was often muffled by the screaming of the wind.

"Wouldn't be surprised if we lost the picture," Libby said. "The way this wind's howling, it's a mercy anything stays standing." At that moment all the lights went out and the TV went blank. Libby flinched as Robin's fingers dug into her arm. She loosened Robin's grip and held her hand as they lay in the dark, hoping the power would be restored. Finally Libby said, "If the lines are down, there's not a chance they'll be able to get them up again until it stops snowing. I guess I'll have to get up and build a fire in the fireplace. Lucky this house was built before the days of central heat, and everybody needed a fireplace in his bedroom." She fumbled in her bedside drawer for a flashlight, then swung her legs over the side of the bed, and felt for her slippers.

"I'll come with you," Robin said.

"I'll be all right, doll baby."

"I don't want to stay here in the dark by myself."

"All right. You can help me bring up some more firewood."

They shuffled their way down the stairs, Robin holding on to her grandmother's sleeve. On the freezing back porch they each gathered an armload of firewood and took it upstairs, shivering. In the bedroom they laid a fire and Robin fussed over getting it going properly, while Libby brought more blankets from the linen closet and spread them on the bed.

"I can't believe how fast the house gets cold when the heat's off," Robin said. "How did people live here in the winter without furnaces?"

"Hardier stock," Libby said. "And more clothes and fires. I doubt it was easy. Come on, let's get in that bed. I bet a lot of children in those big families were conceived in the winter by people just trying to get warm."

They lay watching the firelight flicker on the walls. The dozy sound of logs crackling in the fireplace contrasted with the wailing of the wind outside.

"It feels safe in here," Robin whispered.

"Safe as anyplace I can think of," Libby said.

After a long silence Robin asked, "Have you ever seen anybody die?"

There was a pause as Libby, aware of Robin's need, asked for help in finding the right words.

"Yes. I've seen two people cross over. It's an odd feeling."

"Who?"

"My mother was one. It was like she just slept herself away. Her breathing got slower and slower, with longer pauses in between each breath, like she was doing something important and kept forgetting to take another breath. And then she did forget. Just didn't take another one. It seemed very gentle and easy."

"Who was the other one?"

"Oh, that was a hard one. For me, not for him. My Herb. I'd just put dinner on the table and called him to come. He got up from his chair, put the paper on the floor, where I always had to pick it up. I must have told him a million times not to put that paper down on the floor. He was coming to the table and all of a sudden he just fell down. I thought he'd tripped over something and I almost laughed, but then I saw how still he was, so I ran over to him and he was gone. Just like that. One second he was there and then he wasn't. I couldn't have told you how his last breath was different from any of his others. I didn't pick that paper up for weeks."

"I hope that's how it is for me."

"I hope so, too, honey. For me, too."

In the silence Robin said, "I never got to say goodbye to Mama. Not so she could hear me."

Libby sighed. "Goodbyes are important, but it's the living you do with somebody that matters most. That's what you remember. Anyway, maybe she heard you. We can't know."

"Where do you think she is now?"

Libby shifted her position. "I hope she's someplace where she's young and beautiful, the way I always think of her, and that she's with her dad and her brothers and some other good people and that they're all having a fine time and keeping a place warm for me. That's what I hope, and that's what I think is so. But I couldn't prove it in court. It just sounds right to me."

"Sounds good to me, too," Robin whispered. "The worst thing is being alone."

"I won't let you be alone," Libby said, and held her tight.

It was storming again the day Rick began his new course of chemotherapy, and Libby hid Robin's car keys to keep her from driving to Jefferson.

"I know how much you want to be there, honey plum. But think how I'd feel if you were out there in this dreadful weather, all upset the way you are, and something happened to you. I'd never forgive myself. And Rick wouldn't, either. Anyway, he won't be up to company right away. Why not wait until he can enjoy your visit."

Robin had talked to him on the phone the night before.

"I dread thinking how I'm going to feel by this time tomorrow," he said.

"It's worth it, though, if it makes you better," she told him.

"If," he said. It was the first time she'd heard him doubt.

It took several days for the weather to improve enough for Robin to drive, and then she left for Jefferson immediately.

Just before she entered Rick's hospital room, Robin had a flash of fear. What would he look like? She remembered the last time she had seen him in this bed—the way his face had looked, flushed and content in sleep, when she'd left him that morning to slip back to her own room.

She pushed open the door. He lay against the pillow, his eyes closed, an IV line in his arm.

After watching him sleep for a while, she couldn't restrain herself; she took his hand.

He woke with a start and looked at her. "Eighty-three percent of the water used in this country is for agricultural purposes," he said.

"What?"

"Robin? Is that you?"

"It's me. How do you feel?"

"How do you think? Like my veins have been fried and my stomach turned inside out."

"You've still got hair."

"We'll see how long that lasts."

She held his hand against her cheek and they were quiet. Then he said, "You're not sorry, are you?"

"About what?"

"About what happened last week. Right here."

"Oh, Rick, what a question. Of course not. I never will be."

"I'm glad. And I'm glad we didn't wait." He paused. "Did you see my mother out there?"

"I didn't see anybody. Is she here?"

"She's been hovering around most of the time, weeping and wailing all over me. Sure does cheer a fellow up."

"What can I do to cheer you up?"

"Just what you're doing."

The door opened and a short, thin woman with red-rimmed eyes and a Kleenex balled up in one hand looked in. "Oh, Richard, I didn't know you had company."

Robin stood up. "I'm Robin Gregory, Mrs. Winn."

Rick's mother smiled shakily. "Oh, Robin, of course. The little girl from Bennett Rick went to see so much last summer. Well, he's doing just fine." A swell of tears threatened to spill from her eyes.

"He seems to be," Robin said. "He looks good."

"Do you think so?" Mrs. Winn asked, coming to stand by Rick's bed. She reached her hand out and then drew it back without touching him.

"Robin and I are still seeing each other," Rick said.

"Oh?" She turned to Robin and said apologetically, "Since he went off to college I don't know much about what he's doing. Did you come all the way from Bennett to see him?"

Robin nodded. "It's not that bad a drive. Anyway, a long drive never stopped Rick from coming to see me when I was sick."

"You've been sick?" Mrs. Winn asked.

"Uh, yes," Robin said, glancing at Rick. She could tell by the look on his face that he hadn't told his mother.

"I hope it was nothing serious," Mrs. Winn said conversationally.

"Well, actually," Robin started, "I . . ."

"She has the same thing I do," Rick said.

"Leukemia?"

Robin nodded.

Mrs. Winn pressed the wad of blue Kleenex to her eyes and said, "You'll have to excuse me," and fled for the door.

"Oh, dear," Robin said when she had left.

"I guess I should have told her," Rick said, "but it's so hard when she acts like that."

The door opened and an orderly brought in Rick's lunch tray. "Time for your minimum daily requirements," he said, slamming the tray on the bed table and leaving.

"You want it?" Rick asked. "I don't know why they keep bringing it—I can't eat. I'm mainlining lunch." He gestured to the IV, then struggled to sit up. "And even that won't stay put." He grabbed the metal basin on the bedside table and retched weakly into it as Robin's own stomach turned in sympathy. When he was finished and lay back, wiping his mouth with a towel, she took the basin to the bathroom and washed it out.

"I'm sorry," he said miserably.

"For what?" she asked, smoothing his hair.

"I love you."

"Try to sleep. Shall I go so your mother can sit with you?"

"No. I don't want her. It gives me bad dreams to know she's sitting there leaking. I'll sleep better if I know you're here looking all beautiful and healthy." His eyelids drooped. "Keep the bad things away." And his eyes closed.

As she watched him sleep, she wondered how she could have felt so humiliated the one time she'd vomited in front of him last fall, that she'd begged him to stay away until she was better. How could she not have understood the tenderness with which he'd held her afterwards, and the way he'd told her it didn't matter? She didn't care what he did in her presence now as long as he kept breathing.

"Every year we lose about 6.4 billion tons of topsoil to erosion," he said in his sleep.

"He keeps doing that," Mrs. Winn said. Robin hadn't heard her come in. "I don't know what he means."

"I think he's just saying what's on his mind."

"Oh." She sat down on the other side of Rick's bed and took a fresh tissue from her purse.

"Would you like to be alone with him?" Robin asked.

"Oh, no," she said. "Please stay. I'm sorry I left before. I didn't know what to say." The tears brimmed again.

"That's okay. I don't like to think about it, either."

They sat silently on opposite sides of Rick's bed. "One hundred pounds of fertilizer," he said suddenly.

"What?" his mother asked.

Rick opened his eyes and looked first at her and then at Robin.

"You were babbling again," Robin said.

"Oh." He closed his eyes and then opened them again. "How long can you stay?"

"I have to go pretty soon. I'm supposed to be home before dark."

"I can't go back to school this semester. Can you come to Moreland to see me?"

"When?"

"I'll let you know." They sat holding hands for a while longer before Robin rose to go. She leaned over and kissed him goodbye—definitely not the kind of kiss to give an invalid in front of his mother, but she didn't care.

Driving back to the farm, she had to pull over to the side of the road twice until she could stop crying enough to see the lane lines.

Rick wouldn't let her come to the hospital anymore when he was in for treatments; he was just too filthy sick. So she came to The Property, as she had begun to think of it, as often as she could, bringing with her the deepest calm she could generate.

Each time she arrived, Mrs. Winn looked surprised to see her.

Robin distracted Rick with checkers and gin rummy and reading aloud—books that removed them from reality—Tolkien and *The Chronicles of Narnia; Cat's Cradle,* which made him laugh; and Robert B. Parker mysteries.

Often they just sat in the sun-room Mrs. Winn had had constructed on the south side of the big house, holding hands and looking out through the tall curved glass windows at the snow.

Mrs. Winn always hovered in the background, ready to spring forward with a drink, a snack, a pillow, whether one had been requested or not.

Robin met Tad Winn twice. He was a brisk, handsome man who looked more like a businessman than like a farmer. He wore Western-style gabardine suits and cowboy boots and carried a briefcase, which he put down to shake her hand and to tell her how pleased he was that she could come to see Rick, and how special she must be to make the long trip.

After their first meeting, Robin went back to the sun-room and said to Rick, "Your father's not what I expected."

"Don't let that New World charm fool you. It just oozes out of him like oil. He's got another side."

"I believe you. Nobody puts together an operation like this"—she waved her arm to include the acreage beyond the curved windows —"without being tough."

"This is such beautiful land," Rick said. "You know how much I hoped I'd get a chance to run it my way."

"He looks pretty vigorous to me. You'll have to wait a while for him to retire."

"It's not him I'm thinking about."

She took his hand. "You wouldn't let me talk that way when I was sick. You always insisted I was going to get better. And I did. So will you."

"Sometimes you can tell things, things that have changed," he said. "When I was about ten, my father gave me a little safe with a combination lock on it. But he didn't give me the combination. He told me that if I could figure it out, I could keep whatever was inside. One of his little character-building exercises. Well, I went at it. I was going to show him. I must have spent a hundred hours twiddling with that lock. Do you have any idea how many possible combinations there are to a lock like that? Millions. I probably tried most of them. It got to be second nature, whenever I'd sit down to do anything else, my homework, or to watch television, one hand would be fiddling with that lock. One afternoon I was watching TV and fooling with the combination and suddenly I felt the tumblers click together, the barest, smallest movement, but my fingers were so sensitive by then from all the time they'd spent on that lock that they *knew*. Of course, I didn't know what the combination was; I hadn't been looking, but I'd gotten the damn thing open."

"What was in it?"

"A piece of paper that said 'Congratulations. I wondered if you could do it.' And there was a fifty-dollar bill. The point is not the kind of man my father is, but that when you've spent enough time thinking about something, and fooling with it, when something about it changes, you know it, whether anybody else notices it or not. That's how I've felt since January. Something is different now."

"Of course it is. You've been going through a hard course of beetle squeezings. That's enough to unbalance anybody for a while."

"Robin, listen!" he said. "It's not just that. It's something else," he insisted.

"You're going to be fine," she said soothingly. "Do you want me to read for a while? Or we could play Clue. We haven't played that in a while."

Spring

The first day of spring, a blizzard swept down from Canada and took three days to blow itself out. For a week, temperatures stayed below freezing. The sky was a hard crystalline blue, and the billows and crests of snow were crusty and stiff.

On the second of April, Robin woke to the sound of water dripping. She opened her eyes and saw that the icicles in front of her windows were tipped with falling drops of water.

She jumped out of bed and dressed for school. Exploding into the kitchen, she cried, "It's melting!" and gave Libby a big kiss on the cheek. "It's melting, Polly!" she said, twirling over to Polly's cage.

"Robin! Wash the gun!" Polly said. Now that her repertoire was bigger, Polly sometimes mixed her phrases.

"Oh, yes, sugar pie," Libby said. "Isn't it wonderful! I know spring will come every year, I really know it, but there are times during the winter when I wonder."

Robin grabbed a piece of toast as it popped from the toaster, and threw it onto a plate. "What goes with this?"

Libby scooped a poached egg from its water bath and put it on the toast. "Bacon, too, if you want it."

"Yes! And juice. And whatever else you've got!"

"You *are* celebrating."

"Rick goes in for tests today and I just know this is a good omen. Everything's going to be all right now. Once the weather's better, he can get out more and feel more energetic. It's terrible, being cooped up inside. It makes you feel like a prisoner, or one of those crazy relatives people keep locked up in the attic."

"Locked up in the attic?" Libby asked, putting hash browns and bacon on Robin's plate and sliding it in front of her.

"Oh, they do it, don't deny it." Robin's high spirits could not be quenched.

There was electricity in the atmosphere at school, too. The charge of soft air released a winter's worth of laughter, flirting, and general misbehavior, and teachers in every class struggled to maintain discipline and order.

"Earth to Robin," Marci teased her at lunch. "You haven't heard a thing I've said in the last ten minutes."

"Isn't it wonderful? It's spring. I'm in love. I feel like I don't know what . . . like I'm full of stars!"

"For goodness' sakes! That must mean Rick's doing better, too."

"He's having some tests today, but I just know they'll be perfect. I can feel it."

"I'm glad. Remember last summer, Rob? When you pulled that foreigner stunt on me? I never would have guessed in a million years that you were both sick."

"That was a good day." Robin tossed the plastic bags from her lunch in the trash.

"Maybe for you," Marci said as they walked to their

next class. "I felt like an idiot when I found out he understood everything I said."

"It was okay. He loved it. He would have followed you right down the street if I'd let him."

"I'd have returned him. I think you two are supposed to be together."

"So do I," she said, hugging Marci.

After school Robin drove home with the car radio as loud as she could stand it, singing and beating time on the steering wheel. She threw her books on the sofa in the parlor and dialed Rick's number, but all she got was the answering machine.

Libby came down the stairs. "I thought I heard you come in."

"Hasn't it been a beautiful day?"

"Beautiful? It's a mess out there," Libby said. "Everything's dripping and melting and muddy. I was worried you'd get stuck somewhere on the way home."

"On the highway? You worry about the oddest things," Robin said. "I'm starving. What is there to eat?"

"That's not such an odd thing to worry about," Libby said. "My mother used to worry about having her dentures stolen."

They went to the kitchen together to make a snack.

Robin called Rick again at about five, but there was still no answer.

Just as she was finishing dinner, the phone rang. She ran to the parlor and grabbed it. "Hi! Where have you been?"

"Wending our way home. The tests took a long time."
His voice sounded very far away.

"You sound funny."

"You know," he said, "the first time I was in the hospital, over three years ago now, there was the jolliest little old man on the floor. He was always making jokes and cheering everybody else up, even though he was very sick with a terminal cancer. I was still in shock over my diagnosis and I needed some help. So I asked him how he could be so lighthearted and he told me that he hadn't been like that ever before in his life. He'd always lived in fear that he would get cancer. A lot of people in his family had had it and he figured it was inevitable for him, and he'd spent his life being worried and sour and grim. Then, when he finally did get cancer, it was like a relief. The suspense was over and he could relax. He really had a nice personality underneath the whole time. Seems a shame, huh? But I can understand the suspense part. Always waiting."

"Rick, what happened?"

"It's worse. It's spread. There's nothing more they can do."

"What?" She was squeezing the phone so hard her hand ached.

"I told you I knew something had changed, that something was different, but you wouldn't listen. I wasn't even surprised when the doctor gave me the news."

"They have to do something. There must be something they can do. How can they just abandon you like that?"

"Robin, don't."

"But this can't happen." She was too stunned for tears.

"Please. I need you to talk to. Don't deny me that anymore. I don't have enough energy to fight you, too."

"But it's wrong! They have to save you!"

"Robin, the prize is not always survival at any cost. The price can be too high. Sometimes the prize is peace and rest."

"What about all those prayers to those unknown saints? Weren't they listening?"

"Everybody has to die sometime. Prayers aren't a life-insurance policy. Robin, please. You've spent weeks being so cheerful and positive that I couldn't get through to you with what I knew was happening. I can't protect you from my rage anymore. Help me find someplace to put it. Don't be like my parents."

She stopped. What could she give him now? "All right," she said. "Tell me."

He did, until his anger was drowned by his sobs.

She left for Moreland as early as she could Saturday morning. Minutes counted now.

Mrs. Winn answered the doorbell and whispered, "Oh, Robin, Richard's expecting you. Come in." She turned and tiptoed across the wide front hall. Robin closed the door and followed her to the sun-room, where Rick waited in the recliner.

Robin took his hand and kissed it. "Hi."

"Hi, too."

Mrs. Winn tiptoed away.

"Why is she whispering and tiptoeing?" Robin asked.

"Premature mourning. Also, my father's hung over, so she's trying to be quiet. He's not taking this very well."

"Are you surprised?"

"No. I almost have to admire his persistence."

"You miss him, don't you?" she asked.

"Yeah," he said softly. "I miss him."

She sat in his lap and put her arms around him. "What shall we do today?"

"I've got to get out of here. Let's take a picnic and go somewhere."

"A picnic! It's chilly and muddy out there."

"We can take it to a motel."

"Oh."

"I've got to be with somebody who can touch me, Rob. My parents seem to think I'm contagious, or breakable, or contaminated. I'm starved for touching."

She gave him her best smile. "I can supply all the touching you can tolerate. Let's go."

When Rick and Robin went to the kitchen to put together a picnic, Mrs. Winn tiptoed in to help them. "A picnic? In this weather?" she asked.

"We'll eat it in the car if we have to," Rick said. "Or in a movie. I've got to get out of here for a while, Mom."

"Well . . . all right. As long as Robin will bring you home the second you get tired. You sit down, Richard. Robin and I can handle this. You don't want to tire yourself."

They made sandwiches and deviled eggs and wrapped slices of cake and pieces of fruit. Mrs. Winn put in cans of soft drinks and a package of M&Ms. "Is that enough, do you think?" she asked. "When will you be back?"

"It's enough to get us to South America," Rick said. "I don't know. I'll be back when I get back. Don't worry. Robin will take good care of me."

On the way to the car, Rick slipped behind his father's bar in the corner of the living room and extracted a bottle of wine, which he tucked inside his sheepskin coat.

They drove along the wet highway, throwing up sprays of dirty water, between fields whose rich moist brown contrasted sharply with the white that still partially covered them.

"Thanks for getting me out of there," Rick said. He directed her to a Best Western motel along the highway. "It looks okay and it's the closest one. I don't want to waste any time."

After he registered, they carried the picnic basket to the room and put it on the table. Rick investigated the bathroom and closet, tried all the lights and the television. "Everything works," he said. "I guess we can stay."

"What's first?" she asked.

He put his arms around her.

She lay with her head on his shoulder, tensing her throat to keep back tears. He was already much thinner than he had been in Jefferson, and it seemed she could feel the heat radiating from his bones all down the length of her body.

"My mother would croak," he said.

"So would my father."

"I don't care."

"Me, neither."

"You hungry?"

She got up and brought the picnic basket back to the bed. Tucking the covers around her again, she opened it, passed a paper plate to Rick, and filled it with food.

"Your mother makes a terrific picnic."

"I'd rather have the kind of nourishment you give me." She leaned against him, closing her eyes.

"I wish I could die right now," he said.

"Don't say that." She put her fingers over his mouth.

He kissed them. "Why not? I couldn't get any happier than I am right now."

"Then I wish I could go with you. Why should I wait either?"

He sat up and took her by the shoulders. "Don't say such a thing!" he said, giving her a single shake. "You're doing well now and there's so much life left for you! You know how I hate giving it up."

"I'm sorry, I'm sorry," she said, raising her hands to his face. "It's just . . ."

"I know," he said, pulling her against him.

"Libby told me, when I first knew I was sick, that the hardest thing in the world is to watch somebody you love hurt, because there's nothing you can do about it. She's right."

"No. She's wrong. There is something you can do about it. And thank God you're doing it."

She pressed her face against his chest. "It's not enough."

"Yes," he said. "It's enough."

She put on her coat and looked back at the room. "We never drank the wine."

"We didn't need it. I don't know why I thought we would. Let's leave it for the next person."

Robin drove him home late in the afternoon as he slept in the seat beside her.

"I'll be back tomorrow," she told him when he got out of the car.

He leaned back in and caressed her cheek. "It's so much driving."

"I'm coming. We can just sit in the sun-room if you're tired. I'll read to you. But I'm coming."

"Okay. How can I say no?"

At dinner that night Will said, "I've been reading in *The New Farm* about an experimental farm in Pennsylvania. I may be going soft in the head, but I think I'm going to take a few acres and try some of the things they do there. This strip-cropping they use looks like a lot of work to set up, but the payoff in erosion control, weed control, and soil nutrition could be worth it. If it works. Not using any chemicals would save me enough money that I could afford to take a dip in yield, if that happens."

"I think it's a wonderful idea," Libby said. "And I know Rick would be glad to help you. Wouldn't he, Robin?"

"He always wanted a farm he could operate that way," she said.

"Not making any headway with his father, huh?" Will asked.

"I think he's given up on it."

"I'll be glad when he feels up to visiting us again," Libby said.

Robin excused herself and went upstairs. She closed the door of her room and leaned back against it. How could she tell them about Rick? She'd never forget the look on her father's face when she'd told him about her own diagnosis.

There was a tap on the door and Libby's voice: "Robin, let me in."

Robin took a deep breath and opened the door.

"What's going on?" Libby asked, shutting the door behind her.

"What do you mean?"

"One day you're floating around here high as a hawk and the next you're so down in the mouth your chin's hitting the floor."

"Haven't you ever heard of moody teenagers?" Robin asked, her back to Libby.

Libby put her hands on Robin's shoulders. "Is it . . . Aren't you feeling well?"

"I feel fine."

"No, you don't. You're worrying me, doll baby. What is it?"

Robin said nothing.

"Then it's Rick." Under her hands Libby felt Robin tremble. "What?"

So she told her and they held each other with helpless arms. "But you can't tell Daddy," Robin said finally. "Not until we have to."

"All right," Libby said. "If that's how you want it."

She spent the next morning reading to Rick in the sun-
room. They took a slow walk around the farm, where
the snow was now gone except for a few shady spots. In
the stable they visited Rick's horse, Clover, and fed her
sugar and apples. Rick talked to her, apologizing for not
being able to ride her anymore. He promised her a good
sunny pasture as soon as the weather permitted.

"How old is she?" Robin asked.

"Eighteen. Getting old for a horse."

"I'll be eighteen next week. It feels old to me, too."

Rick held her, stroking her back. "Not to me. What
do you want for your birthday?"

"You to be better," she said into his shoulder.

"What else?"

"Nothing."

"Come on. What else?"

"All right. Something extravagant."

Rick laughed. "I've always heard it's the thought that
counts."

The next weekend, they drove to Moreland for Robin's
birthday dinner. Rick gave her flowers and a big gold
box of chocolates and left several other white-wrapped
boxes in the car when they got to the restaurant.

"Aren't we going to bring all those nice presents with
us?" Robin asked. "When do I get to open them?"

"Is this the girl who wanted nothing for her birthday?
Later, G.R. Later."

The restaurant was an elegant one, and Robin had worn
her best dress of thin blue wool. Rick wore slacks and a

sports coat that looked a size too large for him. Sitting across the table from him, Robin observed how sharp his bones seemed, the planes of his face defined in clean angles. Rather than looking gaunt, he looked somehow purified, refined down to his framework.

"I wish we could get married," she said.

"I wouldn't do that to you."

"Why not? Then I could be with you all the time."

"It would be too hard."

"I don't care." She could feel tears rising.

"Don't, Rob," he said, reaching for her hand. "How about if we pretend we're married?"

She willed herself to smile. "If that's the best you can offer."

"No one else has ever had that offer from me." He paused. "Or ever will."

After dinner they went to their Best Western motel and Rick carried in the flowers, the chocolates, and the packages.

"You can open your presents now," he said. "Did you notice I wrapped them in green ribbons?"

"Which one shall I open first?"

"The big one."

The big one contained a plush rooster wearing a collar with a disk that said "Happy." She laughed and kissed him. "Now which?"

He handed her a medium-sized box. In it was an old green baseball cap with a gold patch across the front that said THE NEW FARM. She looked at him. "What's this?"

"It's mine. I got it when I took out my subscription.

Wear it when you're walking the beans. It'll keep your nose from getting sunburned."

"It'll make me think of you."

"That's the idea."

He helped her open the last and smallest box. "It's beautiful," she said, removing a gold chain with a small gold heart on it. Her name was engraved on the front and Rick's initials on the back. He helped her fasten it around her neck. "A heart holds us together," he said.

The next time Robin went to see Rick, he was dozing in the recliner while *Casablanca* played on the VCR.

"Hey, wake up," she said. "It's a felony to sleep during *Casablanca*. At least a misdemeanor."

He opened his eyes and it was a moment before he recognized her. "Robin? Hi."

"Hi, too."

"Was I sleeping?"

"Yes. And during *Casablanca*. I never thought I'd see you do that."

"Maybe I'm finally getting tired of it."

At the end of May, Rick went back to the hospital and Robin had to tell Libby.

Libby got up from her knees where she had been spreading mulch around her new vegetable garden and went to sit on the back steps. She pulled off her gardening gloves and took Robin's hand in hers.

Robin leaned against her. "I'm going to see what I can work out at school. I'll take incompletes in my classes and make up the exams in the summer. Or I'll do the

assignments on my own and try to take the exams in
June. But I can't sit in a classroom and know Rick's in
Jefferson and I'm not with him."

"Don't even think about school. You have to be with
Rick. You have to be. The worst thing is being alone."

Robin nodded.

"We'll have to tell your dad now. He keeps talking
about Rick getting well enough to come over and see what
he's done."

Robin sighed. "I can't believe this is happening." She
stood up. "I'm going in to call my teachers."

Every morning, Robin drove to Jefferson. She stayed
all day, sitting most of the time by Rick's bed, and in the
evening she drove home again.

To Robin's surprise, Rick's father spent almost as much
time with Rick as she did. At first he sat mutely, watching Rick. On the fourth day, he reached out and took
Rick's hand. Rick opened his eyes, looked at his father,
smiled, and closed his eyes again. From then on, whenever Mr. Winn came into the room, he sat down and
took Rick's hand.

Mrs. Winn forced herself to stand by Rick's bed for a
few minutes every hour, then retreated to the lounge,
where she wept until it was time for her to come to his
room again.

The only times Robin left Rick were for trips to the
bathroom, the cafeteria, or to look at the babies in the
nursery. They no longer looked raw and unfinished to
her, the way they had the first time she'd been in the
hospital. Now they looked fresh and promising, a new

crop of people starting out. Some would be straight and
strong and others would develop poorly, the way some
plants did, even in the same soil. It was a mystery.

Mr. Winn stood up and stretched. He and Robin had
been sitting silently by the bed for several hours, each of
them holding one of Rick's hands while he slept. He was
propped up all the time now to help him breathe and he
had been on oxygen for two days.

"I'm going to get something to eat," Mr. Winn said to
Robin. "I won't be too long. I know you have to start
for home soon."

"It's okay. Take all the time you need."

He bent over Rick. "I'll be back soon, son."

Rick opened his eyes. "Bye, Dad."

"See you later." He left the room.

Rick turned his head on the pillow to face Robin. "Hi."

"Hi, too."

" 'Goodbye, world . . . goodbye to clocks ticking . . .
and Mama's sunflowers. And food and coffee. And new-
ironed dresses and hot baths . . . and sleeping and waking up. Oh, earth, you're too wonderful for anybody to
realize you.' "

"What's that?"

"Our Town . . . Thornton Wilder . . . It was our . . .
high school senior play. That's the . . . quote of . . .
the . . ."

"Rick?"

The image of red taillights leaving her driveway that
lost night in June came into her mind.

Summer

Robin walked down a row of soybeans, Rick's *New Farm* cap shading her face. She loved to look around her and see all the green. Somewhere she had read that there were thirty-seven shades of green, and looking at the fields, she believed it.

She stood under the oak tree where she and Rick had sat that first day, and thought of all the years of planting and growth and harvest these fields had seen, and all the ones to come. With care, the cycle would go on and on and on.

She sat down and leaned against the tree, thinking of a game her mother had played with her when she was little, a game they called The Worst Thing. When Robin didn't want to do something, or was afraid of doing it, her mother would say, "What's there to be afraid of? What's the worst thing that could happen?"

When Robin resisted going to school her first day, her mother asked her that. And Robin said, "Nobody will like me. The teacher will be mean to me."

Her mother said, "And then what? If the teacher's mean to you, I'll go talk to her and tell her to stop. How could it be that nobody will like my angel baby? But if that's what you think, we'll invite them all out to the farm and let them jump in the hay and play with the new kittens and have ice cream and cookies for lunch. That'll change their minds. So what is there to worry about?"

When Robin was afraid to go on stage for the first-grade play, her mother asked her what was the worst thing that could happen.

"I could forget my lines and stand there and everybody will laugh at me."

"And then what? Then the teacher will whisper your lines to you and you'll say them and everybody will stop laughing, if they were even laughing to start with. Most people know the very same thing could happen to them and they're pretty nice about it. So what is there to worry about?"

When Robin didn't want to go to bed at night, her mother would ask her why, and Robin would say, "I'll lie there and lie there in the dark and not be able to go to sleep."

"And then what? Eventually you'll fall asleep."

"And you and Daddy will do something fun without me."

"And then what? We'll tell you about it in the morning. Or, if it's really, really fun, we'll wake you up so you can do it with us. So what is there to worry about?"

Now Robin had to play the game by herself. The best thing that could happen would be that she got well. Of course that's what she wished for. And the worst thing? That she would die.

And then what?

Either she would be someplace or she wouldn't. If she wasn't anyplace, if it truly was lights out, the end, eternal sleep, then what was there to worry about? If she *was* someplace, then Rick was there, too. And Julie and Herb and lots of other people. And so there was still nothing to worry about.